HOW TO
BECOME
A PLANET

HOW TO BECOME A PLANET

NICOLE MELLEBY

Algonquin Young Readers 2021

Published by
Algonquin Young Readers
an imprint of Algonquin Books of Chapel Hill
Post Office Box 2225
Chapel Hill, North Carolina 27515-2225

a division of
Workman Publishing
225 Varick Street
New York, New York 10014

LIBRARY OF CONGRESS CATALOGING-IN-PUBLICATION DATA
Names: Melleby, Nicole, author.
Title: How to become a planet / Nicole Melleby.
Description: Chapel Hill, North Carolina : Algonquin Young
Readers, 2021. | Audience: Ages 9–12. | Audience: Grades 4–6. |
Summary: "After an entire summer trying to figure out how to go back
to being the person she was before her depression and anxiety diagnosis,
twelve-year-old Pluto finds out—with the help of the Hayden Planetarium
hotline, a new tutor, and a new friend—that there is no old or new
Pluto, there's just Pluto, growing up"—Provided by publisher.
Identifiers: LCCN 2020039373 | ISBN 9781643750361 (hardcover) |
ISBN 9781643751627 (ebook)
Subjects: CYAC: Depression, Mental—Fiction. | Anxiety
disorders—Fiction.
Classification: LCC PZ7.1.M46934 Ho 2021 | DDC [Fic]—dc23
LC record available at https://lccn.loc.gov/2020039373

10 9 8 7 6 5 4 3 2 1
First Edition

FOR LIZ,
BECAUSE I PROMISED HER OUTER SPACE.

In 1964, two astronomers at Bell Labs in New Jersey started testing a horn-shaped radio antenna. They wanted to detect the natural radio waves produced by gas clouds in space.

Instead, they encountered something they couldn't explain—low-level energy, coming evenly from all directions in the sky.

Without realizing it, they had made one of the most profound discoveries in human history: Light from the big bang itself, released when the universe was only 380 thousand years old, less than one hundredth of one percent of its current age.

–TIMOTHY FERRIS, *DARK UNIVERSE*, THE AMERICAN MUSEUM OF NATURAL HISTORY

HOW TO BECOME A PLANET

CRITERION #1

A PLANET MUST ORBIT THE SUN.

Pluto was on the phone with the Hayden Planetarium Astronomy Question and Answer Hotline, trying to find out how to create a black hole, when her mom broke down Pluto's bedroom door.

Pluto wasn't allowed to lock her door, but that night the rule didn't stop her. She needed to keep everyone, everything, out so she could just . . . just stop. Just turn off the lights and shut her eyes and *stop*, which was something she had been thinking more and more about lately.

Hence, the black hole.

But she couldn't do that, couldn't stop or think or anything, with the way her mom was pounding on the door, shouting over and over, *"Open the door, Pluto! Let me in! Just open the door!"*

The voice on the other end of the phone was jovial and kind as they explained how black holes were created. But that wasn't right, wasn't what Pluto wanted. She knew how black holes were created in space. She knew that it took a dying star, an explosion, and a gravitational game of tug-of-war.

That didn't help her here, now.

Pluto felt heavy sadness, a weight that pushed down on her chest, and she could hear her mom sobbing as silent tears fell down Pluto's cheeks. That weight, and Pluto's reaction to it, was too much. Too dramatic. It was too dark in her bedroom, when it was sunny and spring through her window. She was too shut down for someone who confided everything to her mother.

Her mom's voice, outside the door: *"Pluto, please. Please open the door!"*

The muffled voice on the other end of her phone: "Can we help you with anything else today?"

Pluto's head rested against her cold wall, light gray and plastered with little glow-in-the-dark stars she had tacked on with her mom when she was four. She picked at one with her thumbnail, pulling it off and taking bits of gray paint with it. She couldn't explain what happened next, only that the sadness turned to anger in her chest, and she knew those little stars wouldn't help her. They wouldn't die and explode and suck her into their dense nothingness, and she was mad at them. She was mad at those little stars, and at the voice on the other end of the planetarium hotline, and at her mom, and at herself, and she needed the stars to come down. She needed them to stop glowing.

She dropped the phone and ignored her mom, and she pulled at those stars, one by one, yanking paint off the wall and throwing them away. It still wasn't enough to make everything stop, and she reached for the books on her bookcase, the astronomy ones her mom had bought her every year for her birthday, and she threw them, too, reveling in the sound of hard thumps as they hit the walls and the floor.

She reached for her brand-new book, too, the one about the *Challenger* sitting on her desk next to her mom's old computer, the one her dad had sent to try to make her feel happy, which was ridiculous, really. The *Challenger* was a tragedy, and Pluto had enough of her own sadness lately. She held the book up as high as she could, but before she could launch it across the room, she heard a loud, splintering crack—which was just as satisfying, really—like something huge crashing *down, down, down.*

But it was just her wooden door, and then her mom's arms were holding her tight.

When it finally came after one hundred and eighty long days, the first day of summer break didn't matter to Pluto. The countdown she'd made with Meredith still read *34 Days Until Freedom!!!* because Pluto hadn't been to school in over a month. She hadn't had to worry about end-of-the-year pool parties, or endless *have a great summer*s, or Meredith begging her to just *be her friend again*.

And, finally, she didn't need to worry about school calling home, asking where she was, asking when she was coming, making her mom's voice tremble as she spoke into the phone, "I don't know. I don't know. I don't know what to do, either."

Instead, what Pluto did have to worry about was that her mom was already out of the shower, shuffling around in the bathroom they shared, nearly ready to start the day. The hall light was on, bleeding into Pluto's bedroom, making the thick purple curtains that blocked out the morning sun null and void. If she had a bedroom door, she would close it to block out the light and the sound of her mom as she hummed while she got dressed.

But Pluto did not have a bedroom door, and hadn't had a bedroom door for a little over a month now.

Her mom stuck her head in the doorway. "Hey, Shooting Star," she said, words mumbled as she spoke around the toothbrush in her mouth. "You're with me today, kid, so start making some moves."

Pluto and her mom both knew she would not be "making some moves." Pluto resented the fact that her mom even suggested it, that her mom went about her morning as if nothing had changed inside Pluto, as if an endless month in bed could suddenly come to a stop without trouble.

When she didn't move: "Plu, I'm serious." As if that made a difference.

Pluto was serious, too. She needed to stay in bed, under her thick purple blanket covered in white little stars. Her mom had picked out the bed set the moment Pluto outgrew the small wooden crib with the solar system mobile.

The blanket was warm, and it was soft, and it was not something she was willing that morning, or any other, to give up.

The bed shifted as her mom climbed in, smelling like the Taylor Swift perfume Pluto had bought her for Christmas last year. Her mom's arms wrapped around Pluto's middle, holding her close against the scratchy fabric of one of the low-cut tops her mom always wore that Pluto hated. Her mom's breath tickled her ear. "I don't want to pay for a sitter, Pluto. I want you to come with me."

Pluto felt a familiar feeling rise from her stomach up into her throat, one that made her want to scream and cry and argue, if only she weren't so tired. Tears came anyway. Twelve-year-olds couldn't stay in bed all day on their own, no matter how much they might need to. If she was older, an adult, she would stay in bed and no one could force her to do anything, a fixed planet around which everything else moved while she ignored it. But for now, Pluto was the moon and her mom was the planet she was forced to orbit.

Even if that meant being pulled out of bed, every inch of her silently protesting, while an invisible rubber band that kept her body strapped down was yanked taut as her mom tugged her into sitting. "There's my girl," her mom said, as Pluto blinked at her slowly. Her mom's eyes were gray, like clouds during a rainstorm, and while they were always so gentle when they looked at Pluto, they hadn't wrinkled at the corners with a genuine smile in what felt like forever. That, though, was comforting, because Pluto could not remember the last time she really smiled, either.

"Get dressed," her mom said simply, as if she wasn't asking her to do something that required a Herculean effort on Pluto's part. "I'll go make you something to eat. It's the first day of summer, Plu. It's time to start having fun again."

She left Pluto alone to fight the urge to curl into herself and sleep. Standing hurt. Looking over at the *Challenger* book still placed on her desk with the ripped spine hurt. She picked it up, and the cover and first handful of pages slid away from the rest. Even broken, it was heavy in her hand, which was heavy on her arm, which was heavy on her shoulder. Gravity, it seemed, was extra hard on Pluto.

In fairness, gravity had been harder on the *Challenger*. The shuttle had fallen from the sky before it was even close to orbit. It all happened so quickly, the smoke and the explosion and the destruction. Pluto often wondered about what that moment had been like, the one after everything was okay, but before everything was not okay, where the *Challenger* and the seven lives on it were somewhere in between, not okay but not *not* okay.

Pluto called the Hayden Planetarium Astronomy Question and Answer Hotline to ask, once. After a brief moment of absolute silence, the voice on the other end of the phone quickly launched into a detailed account of all the mechanics of why the *Challenger* didn't have a successful takeoff, which didn't answer Pluto's question at all.

She placed the broken book back on her desk and reached for her phone instead, the one she got for her tenth birthday "just for emergencies" but mostly used to download podcasts and, at the time, text back and forth with Meredith.

There was a notification that one of her favorite astronomy podcasts had a new episode about meteoroids, comets, and asteroids waiting to download.

Pluto knew a lot about meteoroids, comets, and asteroids already. She knew that when objects speed into Earth's atmosphere, the heat produces a streak of light from the trail of particles they leave in their wake.

She looked over at her bedroom wall, at the little white specks left in the gray paint from where she'd yanked off the plastic stars one by one a month ago, hearing her favorite podcast narrator in her head: *Like an asteroid, Pluto Jean Timoney leaves a trail of her own destruction in her wake.*

"Pluto!" her mom called. "Don't forget your meds!"

The little orange bottles sat right on top of her desk, next to the broken book. *Take 1 with food. Take ½ in the morning. Take 1 as needed.*

Depression and anxiety. Two words. One brand-new diagnosis.

3

The bell above the pizzeria door jingled as they stepped inside. "Kiera! We're here," her mom shouted. They'd hired Kiera, a college student, for the summer, and she was tasked with opening up.

Kiera was either the tall pretty one with the long, long black braids, or the shorter pretty one with the sea-green eyes. When she was younger, Pluto used to love the older girls. She would follow them around and cling to their server aprons and let them lift her into their arms as she twirled their ocean-salted hair around her fingers. But at the end of the summer they would always leave, and they would rarely come back. She didn't know why it hurt as much as it did, but she decided it hurt less when she didn't bother learning their names.

"We're back here!" Kiera called from the kitchen.

Which meant Donna was there already, too.

Donna was also Pluto's fault, and of all the changes in the past month, Donna was the one that Pluto fought hardest against. Pluto's mom wouldn't hear any of it. "I need help if I'm going to be able to figure out what's best for you and still run the restaurant," her mom had said. "So, Donna stays. Because I need her."

Donna wasn't a Timoney, and she was the first person who wasn't a Timoney to ever run Timoney's Pizzeria. Pluto didn't like how she changed the way their menus looked ("The old ones were a little too difficult to read"); she didn't like how she hovered by the cash register when the new college girls were using it ("They make so many careless mistakes, we should consider confiscating their cell phones"); and she didn't like how Donna made Pluto sit at the counter instead of a booth when Pluto was there for lunch ("Leave the booths free for the customers, Pluto").

And she didn't like how her mom seemed to just give in to any and all of Donna's changes.

Her mom didn't seem to mind, though. If anything, she seemed eager to share the responsibility. When Pluto's mom was a little girl, she'd wanted to be an astronaut.

She'd wanted to touch the stars and look into that vast unknown and uncover it. She'd wanted to step on the moon and leave behind her footprint. Space offered an endless array of possibilities, and Pluto's mom wanted the chance to explore every single one.

Instead, she ran a little pizzeria on the Keansburg boardwalk.

Pluto's great-grandfather had bought the New Jersey hole-in-the-wall that would become Timoney's Pizzeria in 1956. When he died, he left it to his oldest son, Pluto's poppy, and when Poppy died when Pluto was five, he left it to his only daughter. Pluto figured Poppy thought he was doing her mom a favor, like his dad had done for him. Pluto's mom practically grew up in that pizzeria. She was taught how to count using the money in the register, learned fractions from the pies themselves.

But Pluto knew her mom still had dreams of NASA, even if her talking about going back to school happened less and less and hardly at all anymore.

Pluto didn't remember much about Poppy. She remembered he smelled like oregano and oil—just like her mom—and that they both had the same too-many-teeth smile. She remembered he always wore a Rangers hat, and how any time she threw a tantrum (of which there were many), he picked her up with his large hands under her armpits and set her in the "penalty box," which was any isolated corner.

She remembered how he used to tell her, when she was small enough for him to lift onto the counter next to the register, that her grandma sometimes had tantrums she couldn't control, too.

"Did she have to sit in the penalty box?" Pluto had asked.

Poppy had laughed at that.

But both he and her grandma were gone, and the penalty boxes were traded for antidepressants.

Kiera came out from the back kitchen (she was, as it turned out, the college girl with the braids), with Donna trailing her. "Hey, guys!" Donna said, smiling bright in a way that reminded Pluto of a "mom smile," even though Donna didn't have any kids.

"Hey, D, sorry we're late," Pluto's mom said. "I'm glad you're here. I didn't think you were coming in today."

Donna waved off Pluto's mom's concern with the dirty rag in her hand. She was a tall woman, with wide hips and thick dark hair and brown eyes. She had moved to the Jersey Shore from Staten Island a year ago and seemed more at place in an Italian pizzeria than Pluto and her mom (with their blond hair—bleached in her mom's case—and light eyes, regardless of their heritage) ever did. "I forgot

I scheduled an early delivery someone had to sign for. I didn't want to make you rush in," Donna said.

"You didn't have to do that. We'd have gotten here."

Donna looked doubtful. Pluto *was* doubtful.

"It was really no problem. But you want to come help me bring the crates in so I can head out and Kiera can get the tables set?" Donna asked, motioning toward the kitchen where the deliveries were brought in from the back door.

Pluto's mom placed a hand on Pluto's head, playing with the semi-greasy strands of her ponytail. Pluto hadn't taken a real shower in a few days. "I've got your workbooks in my bag if you wanna start looking at those?"

Thinking about those workbooks made Pluto's stomach hurt, made her want to curl into a ball, into the dark, and disappear.

There were thirty-four days of school Pluto had not attended. There were more than thirty-four phone calls made home. There were two home visits, and three different doctor's notes, and endless arguments between Pluto's parents.

But a deal had been made so Pluto wouldn't have to repeat the seventh grade come September, and her mom would no longer be in trouble. That deal involved a tutor throughout the summer, workbooks and lessons, and a whole lot of studying Pluto did not want to do. *Could* not do. *Would* not do, full stop.

Just thinking about it made her feel sleepy, and weighed down, and made her chest tight. Too tight.

"Oh! Anna, before I forget," Donna said as Pluto's mom began pulling the stack of workbooks out of her large shoulder bag and Kiera pulled the cleaning supplies out from under the front counter to start wiping down tables. "Julie next door said they're doing one of those wine-and-paint nights at the pavilion. She and Barb were going to try to get all the business owners together to go. I figured we could schedule a couple of our better girls for a few hours that night so we could join in."

Pluto's mom's smile was tight. "Yeah. Maybe."

"We could use a night to ourselves," Donna said. She was looking at Pluto when Pluto glanced up at her.

Pluto's mom didn't drink, and she wasn't exactly the wine-and-paint-night kind of person, anyway. She was the attend-Comic-Con or binge-watch-*Star-Trek*-on-Netflix kind of person. She was the kind of person who'd met Pluto's dad at a renaissance fair upstate. Pluto's dad loved role-play and games—he still met with his Dungeons & Dragons group every Saturday, which was why he usually couldn't take Pluto for entire weekends. And Pluto's mom had gone dressed up as a member of *Star Trek*'s Starfleet who got lost traveling through time.

Donna was wrong if she thought Pluto was the reason her mom didn't seem enthused by the idea, but Pluto wasn't going to say so.

"Hey," Pluto's mom said, bumping Pluto with her hip. "Get a move on with those worksheets, okay? Sit anywhere you want."

Her mom said things like that a lot. *Get moving, get a move on, move, move, move.*

Her mom and Donna disappeared into the kitchen, and Pluto slithered into the closest booth, not caring that Donna would probably make her move to the counter. The cushioned seat, red and plastic and only comfortable because it was familiar, was ripped at the corner, fuzz poking out from its insides. She put her worksheets down on the table, slick from the cleaner Kiera had wiped it with. Pluto put in her earbuds, then pulled at the fuzz and scrolled through her phone to find her favorite astronomy podcast.

Would bacteria from pizza grease survive in outer space? Pluto provided narration to her imaginary podcast. The Hayden Planetarium Astronomy Question and Answer Hotline, when she'd called them, didn't have an answer to her pizza grease question. Instead, they told her all about the microbes that thrived on the Space Station.

NASA says the International Space Station is covered in bacteria, so why don't we send up a slice from Timoney's to test this grease theory? Pluto pulled her earbuds out again, suddenly uninterested in listening to an actual podcast, and ran her finger over the slick table before wiping the wet disinfectant residue from her hand onto the cushion.

The cushions were made of fuzz, the pizzas were made of dough, sauce, and cheese. Above them—and around them—the universe was made of stars and rocks and galaxies. Her mom always wanted to know what was beyond those stars and suns and rocks and galaxies, and Pluto did, too. Only, lately, Pluto just wanted to know what was beyond the skin and blood and bones and what was inside the brain that made *her*. She just wanted to know what made her want to *stop*, when everyone else seemed so eager to keep moving.

The Hayden Planetarium Astronomy Question and Answer Hotline probably couldn't answer that for her, either.

The bell above the door jingled. It was still pretty early, so Pluto assumed another college student or Martin, their cook, was arriving to work. When she looked up, though, there was an actual customer standing there, one who looked about her age, dark frizzy hair, wild from the ocean air, surrounding her like a cloud. She wore a white T-shirt and long bathing suit shorts that were neon green—Pluto thought she might get a headache if she stared too long. She met Pluto's gaze with ice-blue eyes that were just as bright as those shorts.

When she saw Pluto, she lifted her hand in a small wave. Pluto quickly looked away, searching for Kiera, who had disappeared from the main room, probably to help Pluto's mom and Donna with the deliveries.

Luckily, Pluto's mom appeared from the kitchen and said, "Hey, sweetheart, I'll be right with you," before disappearing again. But then just as quickly as she had gone, she popped back out again. "Actually, Plu, can you help her out, please?"

Pluto's eyes were wide and pleading as she looked over at her mom, whose eyes echoed Pluto's desperation. The hope that shone in them made Pluto want to scream, and cry, and beg her mom to leave her be. Especially when the point of hiring Donna in the first place was for moments like these, where her mom couldn't be in two places at once.

Still, Pluto nodded, and with a relieved smile, her mom disappeared behind the kitchen door once again.

Pluto slowly slid out of her booth and approached the

register, and the customer in her bright neon shorts followed. Pluto kept her eyes down and picked up a pen and pad to take her order. She dropped the pen, and it rolled right near her feet, but that still felt too far away to pick it back up again. Pluto looked around for a new one as she waited for Neon Shorts to speak. When she didn't say anything, Pluto looked up.

Neon Shorts was staring right back at Pluto. "Are you ready?" she asked. "I just wanted to make sure you were ready. I wasn't sure."

Pluto averted her gaze, again, and slowly nodded.

"I just need a large plain pizza."

A large plain pizza was its own button on the register. It was their most popular and easiest order. Still, Pluto stared at the notepad, at the pen in her hand that should have been writing down the simple order. At the very least, she should be punching the button at the register to ring Neon Shorts up, so Pluto could take her money, and make her leave, and get the entire thing over with.

"Are you okay?" Neon Shorts asked, and Pluto recognized the tone in her voice. It was the same one Meredith used when she started changing her mind about wanting to hang out. When Meredith was slowly realizing things were different with her best friend. "I mean, you just seem . . . I just need the one pizza."

Pluto wanted to tell this neon shorts–wearing kid that she didn't mean to make things awkward, just like she wanted to tell Meredith she didn't mean to stop being her best friend. She wished everyone could understand that she just wanted to be in her bed, that she didn't want to talk to people, didn't want to be there helping her mom, and that every part of her body ached in a way she couldn't explain every time she had to *get a move on*. Her body seemed angry, too tired and sad, and was fighting her every step of the way.

Sometimes that anger fought its way from Pluto's body into her chest and up her throat, and she couldn't help that either, but none of that had to do with this kid standing in front of her.

"Should I wait for your mom?" Neon Shorts asked. "It's okay if you don't know how to take my order."

I do know how to take your order. I know how to do all the things, and your shorts hurt my eyes. Pluto wanted to tell her that, but sometimes it was just . . . too hard and too tiring to get her brain and her mouth to work together.

It was no surprise when Neon Shorts lost her patience. Pluto didn't know if she was relieved or disappointed when she said, "Never mind. Don't worry about the pizza."

Before Pluto could find the drive to say, *Don't go! I'm sorry, our pizza is the best but the doctor diagnosed me as broken,*

Neon Shorts was back out the door, the bell above it jingling her goodbye. The pizzeria seemed a little darker with her gone.

That night, as Pluto's bed was pulling her into it as if it were the central point of Earth's gravity, her dad called. Her mom answered from the living room, but Pluto did not have a bedroom door, so she could hear everything.

Pluto braced herself, hoping their conversation would carry on long enough that her dad wouldn't ask to speak to Pluto, too. He lived in the city with his girlfriend and his closet full of business suits and weekends full of D&D. He sent her birthday cards with the writing done by Hallmark, signed simply, "Love, Dad." He took her out to dinner once a month and ordered so much food they chewed more than they spoke. And that was before she'd been labeled with *depression*.

Pluto rolled over, facing the light gray wall with the chips from where she'd removed the plastic stars. It was hard to know what to say to her dad on a good day. On days like this, it felt much too hard to try.

She heard her mom sigh and move away from the doorway, as if that did anything to hide the conversation. "She's still just not . . . herself."

I am, thought Pluto. *I'm right here.*

"No, I know. It's not that, I just could really use your help paying for it," her mom said, her voice hitting a desperate twinge that made Pluto's chest feel tighter. "The tutor is supposed to be great. She's supposed to know how to handle kids like Pluto. And she's right here, in Keansburg. I really think Pluto should still stay right here."

Her mom and dad had been having that fight more often. The one where he said, *She is better off here where I can get her help,* and her mom said, *Please don't take her away from me.*

Pluto would not listen to her mom begging her dad to stop asking to take Pluto away. But before she could drown out the sound with a podcast, the desperate note in her mom's voice disappeared, and she sounded weary and small and tired as she said, "Do you really think it would be better for her there? It wouldn't be too big of an adjustment?"

Pluto couldn't breathe as her mom continued, saying, "I just want my girl back. She's just not my girl anymore."

Pluto pressed play. Turned the volume all the way up, but it wasn't enough.

She wished she had a door to slam shut, even if she couldn't have gotten herself to move from her bed to do so.

4

Some mornings were different, and Pluto knew the moment she woke that this was one of them. Her body did not ache in protest as she sat up in bed, and her heart was racing in a way that suggested she could *get a move on*. A note sat on the dresser beside her, a checklist that her psychiatrist had suggested she make when she and her mom visited at the start of the month.

- Take your medication
- Drink water
- Eat (particularly something healthy!)
- Brush your teeth

- Take a shower
- Do something you enjoy

It seemed simple enough, but some days she couldn't check off anything more than taking the medication her mom practically shoved down her throat. Pluto tucked a greasy strand of hair behind her ear. Today she felt an overwhelming need to complete everything.

Particles can never travel faster than the speed of light, but we could test that theory, here, with how quickly Pluto Jean Timoney can accomplish basic tasks.

Next to the checklist was a glass of water and that morning's medication. One pill to help with the depression, and half of another to help with anxiety.

She took her pills, drinking the water as fast as she could (which wasn't anywhere near light speed), and checked both tasks off the list. Her pulse was still racing, though, even though the list was already much shorter. "Mercury, Venus, Earth, and Mars," Pluto said out loud to herself. "These are the planets near our star." Her mom had taught her the rhyme on Pluto's fifth birthday, when the lights went down during her very first visit to the Liberty Science Center's planetarium. Pluto, her heart racing in the darkness of that dome much like it was racing this morning, squeezed her mom's hand tight, her own palm sweaty. Her mom leaned over and began whispering. *"Mercury, Venus, Earth, and Mars, these are the planets near our star. Jupiter, Saturn, Uranus, too. Neptune, Pluto, we can't see you."* By the time she got to the end, to Pluto, this Pluto forgot to be nervous. *"These are the nine planets that we know. Round and round the Sun they go."*

And then the stars turned on, the dome of the planetarium full and bright, and Pluto didn't care about anything else.

Sometimes the rhyme still helped.

When she left her bedroom, heart racing a little less quickly, she found her mom lounging on the worn couch in the living room, her pajamas and reading glasses on, a throw blanket draped over her and a book in her lap, Netflix playing an episode of *Star Trek: The Next Generation* on the TV. Her mom didn't like silence, often filling the living room with the sounds of frequently watched and much adored episodes of her favorite shows.

Pluto glanced over at the clock on the wall. It wasn't yet 8 a.m., but neither of them slept like they were supposed to anymore. "Mom?" Pluto's voice was hoarse, and she cleared her throat.

Her mom, startled, nearly fell off the couch. "Jesus, Plu! You scared me. You haven't said a word in like two days!"

Pluto paused. "Oh," she said, realizing it was true. She held up the checklist. "Breakfast?"

"I went shopping yesterday. Cereal, pancakes, you name it."

Her mom was always painfully eager when Pluto asked for something these days. Pluto turned toward the kitchen.

"Need help?"

Pluto shook her head. Cereal she could handle. At least today.

Her mom followed her into the kitchen anyway. Hovered while Pluto pulled out the box of cereal, and handed her a bowl. Pluto poured the cereal and was grabbing the milk from the refrigerator when her mom spoke again. "So, your birthday's coming up," she said, handing Pluto a spoon. "Do you still . . . I mean, we always go to the planetarium. Are we . . . We haven't done space things together in a while, so I didn't know . . ."

It was true. It had been a while since they'd checked out an astronomy book from the library to read together; it had been a while since she and her mom had watched a documentary—or *Star Trek*—together on Netflix.

Pluto changed the subject instead, the words bursting out of her like a popped balloon. "I don't want to live with Dad."

Her mom looked as though she might cry. "Plu—"

"I'll go to the planetarium with you if I don't have to live with Dad."

Her mom rubbed at her eyebrows, leaning against the counter as if she could no longer hold herself upright. "I'm not . . . It's not set in stone, I just . . . Your dad thinks he could get you better help there. Schedule regular therapy visits. See better doctors."

"Why?"

"Why?" Her mom's voice had a laugh to it that wasn't funny. It made Pluto's chest squeeze. "Don't you miss your friends? Don't you miss . . . God, laughing? Because I miss your laugh, and I miss talking about what you've learned in school and reading with you and seeing you *happy*."

"No," Pluto said, the squeeze in her chest pushing hard, making her tense, making the hand holding her spoon grip harder and harder. *I miss the way you used to look at me before you broke my door down.*

"Meredith's birthday party is coming up, and her mom told me how much she misses you, too. Don't you want to be able to go? To have fun again?"

The metal of the spoon was digging into her palm. "Stop."

"You're *mine*, Plu. You really think I want to give you up?"

"Stop!"

They were both breathing heavily, and Pluto's mom had tears in her eyes, making the gray of her irises look like clouds in a storm. A storm that Pluto had caused. She pushed her cereal bowl away. She wasn't hungry anymore.

A silence fell over them, and usually her mom was the type of person to fill that silence with anything and everything. When the air between them stretched too long, Pluto felt the tightness in her chest, the way her heart raced as she thought about wasted time and the checklist in her hand and the intense need to get it done.

"Can you help me wash my hair?"

The look on her mom's face was pure relief.

There were three main things that scientists looked at when deciding whether or not a planet qualified as a planet. The planet must orbit the sun, it must be big enough for its own gravity to make it round, and it must have cleared its orbit of smaller objects.

Pluto wasn't a planet, but in order for her to be the real, full Pluto—a Pluto without a diagnosis—she needed her own list.

So she wrote one down.

- Take medication
- Visit the planetarium with Mom
- Go to Meredith's birthday party
- Go to 8th grade in September

Was that all? Could she do that?
And what would happen if she couldn't?

5

Asking her mom if she could take a look at her workbooks without her mom nagging first was a bad idea. Pluto realized that once she saw how her mom's face lit up, how she made a big deal of wiping down one of the tabletops in the pizzeria for them to work at, how when Pluto's pen ran out of ink, her mom basically threw four more at her.

(She then needed to take a pen back when she couldn't find one to write down the next customer's order.)

At least Donna wasn't there. It was only Pluto and her mom (and Martin their cook and the college girls) in the pizzeria, just like it used to be.

"Hey, come on, we did these together earlier this year. You know how to do this," her mom said in between orders, tapping her finger on the paper next to the math work Pluto had been staring at for the last five minutes.

Truth was, she did know how to do it. She liked algebra. She liked how there were set steps to solve for x that never changed shape, always gave the same answer, and couldn't decide suddenly that x wasn't the number it was supposed to be. The answer on her worksheet for x wouldn't change, but Pluto was all too aware that maybe *she* did, and she couldn't focus on remembering how to solve for x, could only think about how she had so much work she needed to do, that Mrs. Beckett used to smile at Pluto when she handed back her tests, and what would it be like to have to sit in Mrs. Beckett's seventh-grade math class all over again come fall.

It was a little after lunchtime, and the rush was thinning out. Still, most of the booths were filled with flip-flop-wearing and sunscreen-scented families. The sound of ice in paper cups filled the restaurant as they drank, trying to cool down from the hot June sun. Her mom was busy, even with the help of two servers, but she kept bouncing back and forth nervously between the counter and Pluto, with a money pouch tied around her middle and a dirty red-and-white-checkered rag thrown over her shoulder.

Pluto's eyes drifted away from her math sheet, homing in on the world outside the pizzeria door instead. It was easy to turn her mom off, to let the math work fade away as she watched the boardwalk, just like when she'd sit around watching *SciShow Kids*, her favorite science show on YouTube. She let the algebra drift out of her head, adding imaginary narration: *It is a hot, humid day at the Jersey Shore, but you don't need to feel the heat to be able to tell. You can see, there, the woman walking with her daughter. The daughter is pointing at the shop with vinegar fries, but her mom, with her thick black hair pulled up high on her head, perspiration dripping down her neck, leads her instead toward the ice cream booth.*

"Come on, Pluto," her mom's voice cut in. She picked up Pluto's pen and put it back in Pluto's hand. "What's the next step?"

What was the next step? Pluto had woken up, and taken her medication, and taken a shower, and brushed her teeth, and brushed her hair, and tried to get ready for the eighth grade. She had to do this. She had to pass.

She had to remember how to breathe.

"You know this. Focus. You can do this."

I can't, she thought. *I can't, I can't.*

It is such a hot day that the normally chatty men behind the game booths, the ones that sell tickets to win prizes like salesmen sell cars, are too busy standing in front of their fans to call at the people walking by.

"Ms. Timoney? I think the register's stuck," the college girl behind the counter called.

"I'm hot," Pluto said, looking up into her mom's face. Her mom's cheeks were red with frustration. Pluto's palms were sweaty, making the pen slick in her hand. "It's too hot."

Her mom exhaled, deflating as the air left her lungs. "No, it's not."

And then the bell above the door jingled, and Pluto looked away from her mom to come face-to-face with Meredith Han.

Meredith had on flip-flops and sunglasses that she'd pushed back to keep her thick, dark hair out of her face, and she stood there in the bright blue cover-up that Pluto had in purple, because they'd bought them together.

And she wasn't alone. She was with her mom, who was waving and calling for Pluto's mom, and two other girls from school. Charlotte Jackson and Harper Leiman were best friends like Meredith and Pluto were best friends, and when Pluto's mom said, "Take that table over there!" the two of them ran ahead of Meredith to get their seats.

"Hey, Plu, come here," her mom said, waving Pluto

over as she greeted Meredith's mom. "Take a break, have some lunch with your friends."

Pluto had already eaten the cheese off a slice of pizza an hour ago.

"Hi, Ms. Timoney," Meredith said, and as Pluto came to stand next to (and slightly behind) her mom, Meredith added a quiet, "Hi, Plu."

"Mrs. Han brought the girls here to hang for a bit before they head to the arcade," Pluto's mom said. "You want to go with them?"

Pluto hated that her mom asked in front of Meredith, in front of Meredith's mom, in front of Harper and Charlotte, who were leaning over to listen from their table.

Meredith was chewing on the inside of her lip, something she did when she was worried. They had been best friends since the third grade, when Meredith introduced herself and said, "My mom watched a lot of TV when she was pregnant and named me after her favorite character in her favorite show," and Pluto had responded, "My mom named me after her favorite planet. Well, it was a planet when she was growing up. It wasn't one anymore when I was born, but my mom looked at me and said it was a perfect fit."

"I hope my mom doesn't think naming me Meredith will make me become a doctor," Meredith had replied before scrunching up her nose. "Blood freaks me out."

But even before the night her mom broke down her bedroom door, Pluto was certain she had become a bad best friend. For almost all of seventh grade, she'd ignored most of Meredith's texts, not wanting to talk. She'd turned down all of Meredith's invitations to her house after school, because Pluto just wanted to go home. Her diagnosis came later, but whatever she had let happen between her and Meredith started much earlier.

"I'll go get a couple of pizzas in the oven for you guys," Pluto's mom said, squeezing Pluto's arm and walking away, glancing over her shoulder before disappearing into the kitchen.

Meredith turned to take a seat at the table, across from Harper and Charlotte, leaving a seat open for Pluto. Pluto stared at that empty seat. She looked back in the direction her mom had gone. *Save me*, she wanted to say. *Tell them I can't do this.*

"Pluto, hon, come take a seat," Meredith's mom said.

She let Mrs. Han lead her to the table, where she sat next to Meredith and across from Harper, who was making a mess, as always, with the salt shaker. "Mrs. Beckett said you were sick," Harper said, leaning forward as if inspecting Pluto for potential infections.

When the *Apollo 11* astronauts returned to Earth, they were scrubbed and quarantined, going through a thorough decontamination process to protect the world from any diseases and other germs they might have brought home. It was said to be a humiliating process, and as Pluto sat there under Harper's scrutiny, she felt as though maybe she could relate.

Charlotte kicked Harper under the table. "We missed you at school," she said.

Meredith said nothing.

"So . . ." Harper said, picking up the pepper shaker. "Where *were* you?"

"Harper!" Charlotte said.

"I'm sorry! I just don't understand!" Harper was a big girl with a big mouth, but she used that big mouth to tell off Jeremy Ng when he made fun of Meredith's teeth or Charlotte's hair or Pluto's name, so everyone (but Jeremy) liked Harper anyway. She turned to Meredith. "I thought you were mad at her."

"My mom made these plans," Meredith said, looking down at the napkin she always kept in her lap.

Pluto turned to look for her mom, who caught her eye from behind the counter, and Pluto knew immediately that no, Meredith's mom hadn't made these plans. Pluto's mom had.

And it felt even more like an ambush.

Mercury, Venus, Earth, and Mars . . .

"I . . ." Pluto managed to say, her heartbeat loud in her ears, and all three girls looked at her. She swallowed. "I should go," she said, because she meant it. Harper and Charlotte and even Meredith didn't seem to want her there anyway. She slinked out of her seat before anyone could protest (*would* anyone protest?), catching her mom's eye again and watching as her dark eyebrows creased and her face fell. The checklist Pluto made was in the back pocket of her shorts, and she reached for it, crumpling it up in her fist. She had nowhere to disappear to in the pizzeria, with her friends (*were* they still her friends?) sitting in one of their booths and her mom watching eagerly from behind the counter.

The bell above the entrance jingled in her wake as Pluto stepped outside.

Pluto thought she would be able to breathe easier outside, with the fresh ocean air, the sun on her face. Away from the smell of pizza. Away from Meredith and Harper and Charlotte. Away from her mom.

The boardwalk always felt more like home than Pluto's actual home did. She'd spent so many summers there, summers that started in the spring and blended into fall. She knew the boardwalk better than she knew herself—especially lately—and she loved it.

Or she used to, before. Before Donna started working with them. Before Meredith and Harper and Charlotte started spending their summer without her.

It seemed brighter today. Louder. The wooden planks felt harder under her feet and looked more splintered and worn. The smell of the hot dogs from the Olde Heidelberg across the way made her want to gag, as did the lingering garbage smell from the dumpsters out back. The woman who owned the burrito restaurant next door was yelling loudly at her son, and the line for the lemonade stand on the other side was long, blocking her way to the beach.

Pluto pushed by, bumping into people who shouted back. She made her way to the railing that separated the boardwalk from the sand, and looked out at the umbrellas scattered like mushrooms popping out from the earth, a swirl of brightly colored pinks and blues and reds and yellows that made her dizzy. But no, she was dizzy because she was breathing funny, because she couldn't take a real deep breath, no matter how hard she tried, and that made her nervous, made her breathe even funnier the more she tried not to.

Mercury, Venus, Earth, and . . . Earth, and . . .

She looked at the wrinkled checklist in her shaky and sweaty hands and tried to smooth it out. The list seemed impossible. How was she ever supposed to go to Meredith's birthday party? How was she ever going to be able to go back to school? She couldn't even have a slice of pizza with three of her friends.

"You want a zeppole?"

She turned to find a little boy with one large front tooth and the other one missing as he leaned into her personal space. His cheeks had powdered sugar on them.

Pluto shook her head and closed her eyes and tried to breathe. *Earth, and . . . and Mars.*

"Fallon!" the little boy called, too close to Pluto's ear. "I think she's broken!"

Yes, I'm broken, Pluto thought. *Just let me be broken and leave me alone.*

She kept her eyes sealed tight as she tried to revel in the darkness, the light spots reflecting behind her eyelids like stars, like the dome of a planetarium. She wanted to get lost in them, to let everything else—the crashing waves of the ocean, the chatter of the boardwalk, the screams from the amusement rides—disappear.

She heard someone come running up, pulling the little boy out of the way—"Get out of her face, Tommy"—and

41

taking his place. There was a tentative touch on Pluto's shoulder, and the new voice asked, "You okay?"

No. She wasn't okay. She was having what the doctor labeled *a panic attack*, and she could not remember a single thing he or her mom had told her for how to stop it. Instead, she tried to breathe and tried not to cry and failed at doing both those things. "I'm *fine*," she said through gritted teeth.

"You don't really look fine."

Pluto opened her eyes to come face-to-face with the kid with the neon shorts and ice-blue eyes she'd failed the other day, her long, wild hair blocking the sun except for a halo it created around her head. Her shorts, this time, were neon blue. "Maybe you should sit down. Will that help?"

Pluto didn't respond, but she let Neon Shorts pull her down so that they could both sit on the hard wooden boardwalk. Around them, people kept walking and talking and shouting and laughing, as if the fun of summer was blinding them to the two kids on the sandy boards. Pluto closed her eyes and tried again to take a deep breath.

She felt a hand on her shoulder, but otherwise, neither of them moved.

"The *Challenger* lasted only seventy-three seconds," Pluto managed to say, her voice scratchy.

"What?" Neon Shorts asked.

Pluto shook her head. "Nothing. It's nothing."

Neon Shorts pointed to the crumpled list in Pluto's hands. "What's that?"

"My list."

"Medication for what?"

Pluto shook her head again. "I don't want to talk about it."

"Sorry! Sorry. We can just sit here," Neon Shorts said. "Will that help? Is it helping?"

Pluto nodded, before pulling her knees to her chest.

"I'm Fallon," she said.

Pluto didn't respond, and Fallon didn't say anything else. She also didn't leave, just sat there with Pluto, who rested her head on her knees, as people walked by, as the sounds of the roller coasters on the other end of the boardwalk roared around them, as the ocean crashed behind them. Pluto didn't move, and Fallon didn't leave, until she shifted and said, "Is that your mom? I think she's looking for you. Hey!" Fallon shouted. "Over here!"

And then arms she would know anywhere were pulling her close, and blond hair was tickling her face, as her mom surrounded her, saying, "Hey, Shooting Star, you're okay. I'm sorry. I've got you."

6

Pluto knew it was coming before her mom even opened her mouth. "I just got off the phone with your dad," she said, taking a seat next to where Pluto had been sitting on the couch for the past two hours.

"No," Pluto said, chest tight as the tears came so easily. "No, Mom, please, *no*."

"Wait, hey, shh." Her mom scooted closer on the couch, practically in Pluto's lap before she pulled Pluto into her own. "Hey, listen to me. We need to talk about this. I love you, Shooting Star. You're my *everything*. You know that, right?"

Pluto was her mom's everything, but that was before.

Back when it was her and her mom and their pizzeria, their own universe against the world. She didn't know what they were anymore. "Then let me stay here. I won't run out on my friends again. I promise. I'm sorry."

"I know you didn't mean to hurt them." Her mom ran her fingers through Pluto's hair, then turned to pull the throw blanket over them both. "I also know that this is . . . new. And bigger than us. I just want to do whatever is best for you, and your dad has money that we don't. There are things he can afford that we can't."

"Dad can just send money," Pluto said.

"Yeah, well, your dad's selfish," her mom said, before pinching the bridge of her nose. "I'm sorry. I shouldn't have said that. I *didn't* say that. There are more resources for you in the city, and some change might be good for you. That's what he and I are talking about. That's what we think we can do for you."

"You just want to get rid of me so you can have more free time to go to wine-and-paint nights with Donna," Pluto said, anger building in her chest. "You have her now so you don't need me."

"That's not true and you know it, Pluto," her mom said. "I can't be here for you and be at the pizzeria all the time, that's true. But hiring Donna as a manager had nothing to do with how I feel about you."

Pluto knew that was a lie. Hiring Donna had everything to do with how her mom felt about Pluto, and how she felt that Pluto was becoming too much to handle. Too much to handle alone without Donna, and too much to keep around instead of sending her to live with her dad.

Pluto twisted in her mom's grasp, trying to get her hand into her pocket. She pulled out the crumpled and now slightly ripped piece of paper, her checklist, and sat up straight so she could show it to her. "Here, look. I made a list, like the one we do every day, and I can check things off. If I do it, if I do all of this, please can I stay?"

Her mom's forehead creased, and Pluto was almost certain she had deeper worry lines these days. "The planetarium? Meredith's party? What is this?"

"It's my list. If I do the list, I'm Pluto again, like normal. And then I can stay. Please give me time to do the list. Don't send me to Dad's yet. I need . . . I can do it, just give me time."

Her mom was quiet and still as she looked at Pluto's list. "Meredith's party is at the end of the summer," she said.

Pluto nodded.

Her mom rubbed her eyebrow and then turned to the coffee table, reaching for a cap-less pen sitting in the mug they used for little loose things like paper clips and hair ties. She flattened Pluto's list out on the table. "Okay. So, medication, the planetarium, and Meredith's party. We'll check them off one at a time over the summer and see what you can do. As for school, I've been in contact with that tutor, and I really think she'll be good for you. I have some . . . things . . . to work out with your father about that, but I think it won't hurt to get you started, at least get you to meet her. So I'm going to call and set that up for this week, okay?"

Pluto frowned but nodded.

"And I have something to add. Because we haven't talked to anyone other than at your medication checkups, and I really think it'd be good for you to see a therapist regularly. Our insurance won't cover a ton, but we could do a couple visits before the end of the summer, and maybe we can get you on your dad's insurance, but anyway." Her mom seemed almost out of breath when she finally paused. "What do you think?"

Pluto hesitated. "I have to see a therapist?"

Her appointments with the psychiatrist were so basic. She answered questions about how she felt on her medications. *Are you more hungry? Are you less hungry? Do your arms or legs tingle? Do you still feel sad? How do you sleep at night? How is your energy during the day?*

Simple questions she could answer, but Pluto couldn't

even talk to her best friend. How was she supposed to talk to a stranger?

But her mom nodded, looking so . . . so *hopeful*. And Pluto didn't want her to hire any more people to take over the pizzeria, and she didn't want her mom to decide to send her away.

"Do we have a deal?" her mom asked.

A list was tangible. A list felt real, and Pluto could take it one step at a time, and she could do this, she *could*.

She took a deep breath and agreed. "Deal."

7

Pluto was starting to suspect that "I don't want to pay for a sitter" was actually code for "I don't want you staying home anymore," but in the face of their new plan, the list that Pluto had to complete by the end of the summer, she didn't mind as much.

She did mind, however, when her mom stopped her before she could sit in a booth. "Come help me today. We're short-staffed."

Pluto didn't buy it. "Donna's literally in the back taking inventory."

"Donna is *busy* in the back taking inventory."

"What's the point of hiring another manager if you're still short-staffed?"

"For someone who hates that I hired a new manager, you're sure making a case for me hiring another." Her mom sighed. "Come on, Plu. Help me out here, like you used to."

Those words knocked the fight right out of Pluto. Her mom was right. *Here we have the Timoney Solar System, its two fixed planets orbit in harmony, no collisions. Like it used to be.*

If Pluto was honest, she didn't even really like pizza. She usually just ate the cheese off the top because she didn't like sauce and she didn't like crust, and she didn't like getting greasy pizza juice all over her hands. As far as family businesses go, this wouldn't have been her chosen one, but she knew her mom hadn't really wanted to choose it either.

(*Why* she had to choose it was because Pluto was born when her mom was nineteen, and a lot of the things she once seemed destined for changed after that.)

When Pluto first started feeling different, when she started wanting to stay home, started sleeping more, started avoiding Meredith, her mom did everything she could to stay home when Pluto needed her. Quickly, though, that meant Pluto was getting in the way. Her mom never complained before about spending long hours on her feet, sometimes making the pizzas herself when the cook

50

canceled, sometimes manning the register and waiting tables and cleaning because college students on summer break weren't always reliable. She never complained before about going through bottle after bottle of Taylor Swift perfume to try to mask the smell of grease and constantly failing.

But when she had to close the restaurant more and more often because she couldn't physically do all those things while staying home with Pluto, and she couldn't just leave Pluto alone, either, she had to change things.

So, she did. Starting with new hours at the pizzeria, followed by babysitters for Pluto, followed by a new manager. Even though no one except a Timoney had ever run the place before, and the only person who was supposed to run the place once her mom was done and had enough was Pluto.

Pluto wondered how Poppy or her great-grandfather would feel about Donna. She wondered if they would consider it all Pluto's fault.

Her mom was currently in the kitchen arguing with Martin, who'd started working for them last summer and who came to work smelling like cigar smoke, which gave Pluto's mom headaches.

Pluto was standing by the register, though it was too early for pizza—for the most part. There was always the chance someone would pop in for a 10 a.m. breakfast slice, which made Pluto want to gag. She had a book open that her new tutor wanted her to read ahead of their first lesson (which was just one of a long list of things Pluto was supposed to do before she even met the woman).

Pluto read the first couple of sentences three times before she gave up. She just wasn't paying enough attention. Her head felt too heavy, too foggy, to focus.

"I read that book last year! How far along are you?"

Pluto popped her head up, startled that she had been concentrating so hard on the book she hadn't even heard the bell above the door. Fallon stood in front of her (wearing bright yellow shorts), and Pluto's cheeks immediately grew warm.

"Are you almost done?" Fallon continued. "I didn't really like the ending."

Pluto put the book down. "I'm not really paying attention to any of it right now." She reached for the pad and pen next to the register, keeping her eyes down and focused on the task instead of on Fallon. "Are all your shorts that bright?"

"What?" Fallon asked, looking down at her shorts. "Oh. They're actually my brother's old ones. I never thought about it. I'll have to ask him about them."

"Oh, you don't have to—"

"Forget the shorts." Fallon lifted up the white box Pluto hadn't noticed in her hands, interrupting her. "I, uh, actually brought these for you."

Pluto frowned. "For me?"

Fallon placed the box on the counter, and Pluto opened one of the flaps. The smell of sugar wafted out, and she saw the powdered white coating.

"They're, uh, funnel cakes," Fallon said.

So they were. "Why?" Pluto asked.

Which was, apparently, the wrong thing to say. Fallon reached to take the box back. "If you don't like them, I'll just . . . my brothers will eat them, it's fine."

Pluto didn't know what to say, but just then her mom and Donna appeared from the kitchen. "Oh! Hello," Pluto's mom said, smiling one of her warmest smiles at Fallon. "Our friend from the other day. What brings you by?"

"Funnel cakes," Pluto said.

Her mom reached for the box, opening it up. "Mmmm. Is that right? These look delicious."

"They're, uh, from my dad's—I mean, our shop. The funnel cakes. And zeppoles and stuff." Fallon's face grew pink. "We're new."

"You're next to the arcade, right? Your mom's Leanne Zamprogna?" Donna asked. She already knew every-one on the boardwalk. Pluto's mom knew most of their storefront neighbors from when she was just a child, but she always made a point of introducing herself to anyone new. She was getting a late start with that this summer, though, and Donna had beaten her to it. Pluto figured that was her fault, too.

Fallon nodded. "Yeah, that's my mom. That's us."

"Well, it was very sweet for you to bring this over to us. Can I send you back with a pizza?" Pluto's mom asked.

"Oh, no—uh—thank you, but that's—we're okay," Fallon stuttered. It made Pluto wonder if she was even supposed to be bringing funnel cakes over in the first place. "I just wanted to . . ."

Check on me? Pluto thought.

"Well." Fallon shrugged, with a small little almost-laugh. "You never told me your name."

"Oh," Pluto said, and when nothing else was forthcoming, her mom bumped her hip. "I'm Pluto."

As expected, Fallon narrowed her eyes. "Really?"

Pluto's mom laughed. "My doing, guilty as charged."

The bell above the door jingled as a young man and woman walked in, and Pluto's mom gently moved Pluto aside, focusing on the couple. "Hey, guys, what can I do for you?"

Which left Pluto and Fallon alone, which seemed to

be what Fallon wanted. She leaned in, hesitated, but then said, "I want to talk to you about your list," which was the last thing Pluto was expecting.

Pluto shook her head. "That's . . . private."

"I think we can help each other out. I just . . . can we meet later? I'll be at our shop until four. Can you meet me by the bumper cars after that?"

Pluto was already shaking her head.

"Just—" Fallon let out a frustrated sigh. "*Please.* I'll tell you how the book ends if you want. I'm better than SparkNotes."

Pluto glanced over at her mom, who was taking the couple's order but had an ear facing Pluto. She knew her mom was eavesdropping. It was sort of her specialty lately. "I can finish it myself," she said.

"Well, what about the other stuff?"

"What about it?"

Fallon let out a frustrated puff of air. "Look, just . . . can we meet and talk about this later? *Please?*"

Pluto caught her mom looking at them out of the corner of her eye, and Fallon was looking at her, too, and it was just . . . all a bit too much attention. So, Pluto surrendered, if only to get back to being alone. "Okay. Fine. But not the bumper cars. The quiet side of the boardwalk, instead."

There was relief written all over Fallon's face. "You have a phone?"

"What?"

"A cell phone. I'll give you my number."

Pluto reached into her pocket, but Donna was on top of it like she had a satellite rigged right into the pizzeria to identify cell phones. "Same rules apply to you as anyone else, Pluto," Donna said. "No cell phone use behind the register."

Pluto was about to argue, because this was her pizzeria, not Donna's, but Fallon interrupted, "I'll get your number later. Four, okay? By the visitors booth."

Fallon left, and the couple her mom was helping sat at a table. Pluto pulled the funnel cake box closer, opened it up and stuck her finger inside, tearing off a piece to eat. It was oily and sweet, which was everything good about a funnel cake.

Her mom came over and popped a piece into her mouth. "Look at that, huh?" she said, wrapping an arm around Pluto and giving her a squeeze. "Somebody made a friend."

Pluto glanced up into her mom's face. She looked just as relieved as Fallon.

The quiet side of the boardwalk was at the opposite end of the amusement park, where the shops thinned out and condos took their place. On this end, Pluto could hear the seagulls, could hear the waves lapping against the shore. On this end, people jogged, or walked along with babies in strollers, and everything was much, much calmer.

Pluto used to prefer the other end, where she'd run around with Meredith, begging their moms for tickets to ride the bumper cars and roller coasters, saving up enough quarters to try to win prizes at the arcade. "Once that man leaves, we'll play that machine. Look at how many tickets he's won!" Meredith had said, just last year. They'd made a point of watching the senior citizens who played the arcade games as if they were at the poker machines in Atlantic City. They'd spent most of June watching the same man, gray mustache and tan cap, play the same game day after day, winning more tickets than Meredith and Pluto had won in all of the summers they'd spent there combined.

Meredith wanted to steal his game, win the tickets he had been winning, but he got there before they did every day, and he stayed until after they got too bored waiting. Until one day Pluto got fed up enough to walk right up to him and ask, "Can we *please* have a turn now?"

He didn't seem too happy about it, but Meredith sure did, as he finally vacated that spot.

Pluto couldn't imagine walking up to a stranger and asking them much of anything right now, and she wondered if that man was back at the arcade this summer, playing the same game. She wondered if Meredith was trying to get him to leave again, if she had gotten Harper and Charlotte to help her try.

Pluto put her earbuds in and turned the volume on her phone way up. She was listening to a podcast about how two astronomers in New Jersey (just like Pluto!) made the huge discovery of light from the big bang itself.

(Could her mom, also born and bred in Jersey, have discovered something too, if things had been different, if Pluto were different, if Pluto didn't exist at all?)

Suddenly, one of her earbuds was yanked from her ear. "Hey!" Pluto yelled.

"I was trying to get your attention for like an entire minute," Fallon said. "What are you listening to?" Before Pluto could pull it away, Fallon held up the earbud to her own ear. Her forehead creased. "Is this for school?" she asked.

Now, Pluto did pull the earbud away. "No, it's . . . it's for me. It's just astronomy stuff."

Fallon leaned against the visitors booth, which was

made of wood and painted white, though the paint chips were peeling and coming off on Fallon's T-shirt. "Like space and stuff? I read a book last summer by Neil deGrasse Tyson. It was on my older brother's summer reading list, but I *always* do all his reading because I read fast and he's an idiot."

Pluto felt like she could float away. "Yes! He narrates one of my favorite planetarium shows. My mom and I go every year for my birthday to the Liberty Science Center— have you ever been? It's right in Jersey City, it's not far, but I've memorized the entire script. Did you like the book?" Pluto was a little out of breath when she finished, and she blushed. She never really spoke that much to *anyone*, let alone someone she just met.

Fallon laughed. "I like all the books. Well, that's not really true. My older brother's high school teacher is going to be *such* a bore, if his reading list this summer is any indication." She pulled out a rolled-up paperback that had been tucked in the deep back pocket of her boy shorts.

"I can give you more. Astronomy books, I mean." The words left Pluto's mouth without thinking, and once she heard them, she almost didn't believe what she was hearing. She didn't know Fallon, not really, and she hadn't lent out an astronomy book since she'd loaned one to Meredith in fifth grade, and Meredith decided she would rather read Goosebumps. "I have a bunch about the solar system, but also about rockets. Like the Apollos. And the *Challenger.*"

"I read a book about that one once, too! About the teacher who was on it. It was so sad."

"It *was* so sad," Pluto agreed. "Her name was Christa McAuliffe and she was chosen out of eleven thousand people."

"Yikes! Imagine, getting chosen out of all those people and then . . ." Fallon said. "Anyway, let's talk books more later, okay? I actually wanted to talk to you about something else." She glanced around the boardwalk, and then leaned in to Pluto. "The list."

Pluto felt her chest tighten, and her shoulders grew heavy all over again. "I told you, that's private."

Fallon kept pushing anyway. "Do you have to do all the things on the list by a certain time?"

"The end of the summer, but I don't want to talk about it."

"What happens if you do?" Fallon asked. "If you finish the list, I mean. Do you get something?"

I get to stay here, Pluto thought. *I get to feel like Pluto again.*

Instead, she said: "You wouldn't understand."

This was a mistake. Fallon didn't really want to talk

about astronomy books or Christa McAuliffe, and Pluto didn't want to talk about her list. She wasn't even sure if she wanted to make new friends. She had a hard enough time keeping the ones she already had, and at least Meredith would know better than to pry into Pluto's secrets. Even if Pluto keeping secrets is what made her lose Meredith in the first place.

"I can at least try," Fallon said.

Pluto bit her lip, thinking about Meredith, and her mom, and everyone who did not seem to understand, because they knew who Pluto was before her diagnosis. Fallon, though, never knew the old Pluto. Fallon couldn't tell how broken she was. "If I don't do the things on the list, I have to go live with my dad. In the city. Because he thinks I can get better there. The things on the list will prove that I can be better here," she said, throat scratchy. "I, um. I have depression. That's what the doctors say."

Fallon grew quiet. Pluto felt the pressure in her chest start to grow. She wanted to take it back and not tell Fallon anything, because clearly Fallon could not understand, and Pluto felt stupid. She opened her mouth to take it back, to tell Fallon she had to leave, and go hide out in the pizzeria, in the dark booth in the corner where she could hope that everyone would just leave her alone.

"If I make a list—" Fallon suddenly said, her voice

hardly above a whisper. "If I help you do yours, will you help with mine?"

"You . . ." Pluto frowned. "You want to . . . what? Why? Are you . . . ?"

Are you depressed, too?

"No," Fallon answered, even though Pluto couldn't get the words out to ask. "But I'm . . . different . . . too, maybe. So, what do you think?"

What did she think?

What did she *think*?

She thought it all seemed impossible, both her own list and helping someone else with theirs. She could barely get one done, let alone two, and she didn't want to be distracted.

But also, she didn't want to do it alone. And maybe now, she wouldn't have to.

Pluto took a deep breath and hoped to heck she wouldn't regret it. "Okay. I'll do it. I'll help you."

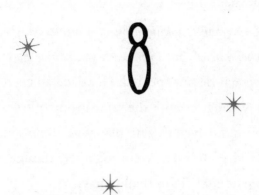

Pluto's phone buzzed four times before she gave in and rolled over to reach for it. She'd spent the entire afternoon and all night in bed, if the time on her phone was actually right, but even as she scrolled through her notifications, she had no plans on leaving the warmth of her blanket.

Her dad had texted twice. Pluto was relieved he was starting to take the hint and texting her instead of calling. It was much easier to talk to him when she could think about what to say first, type it out, delete it if she needed to, try again. *Pluto Jean!* he'd written. Her dad loved exclamation points. *It's almost your birthday!*

Well, yes. That was true. He probably wanted to know what to get her.

My D&D group is taking a bit of a break. Maybe you can spend a weekend here soon. I can teach you how to play!

That was a little unexpected. Her dad had been playing Dungeons & Dragons with the same group of friends since college. Her mom even used to play with them sometimes, when she and Pluto's dad were together, though she was always more of a sci-fi fan than fantasy.

Her other texts were from Fallon, which was also a surprise. Fallon hadn't texted her yet since they'd swapped numbers after Pluto agreed to help her with her list. *Are you going to be at the pizza place today?* and *Maybe I can talk my mom into letting me come hang during my break.*

Meredith used to text her similar things. Texts like, *My mom is bringing us to the boardwalk. I'll come by so we can hang!* Meredith didn't have to ask if Pluto would be at the pizzeria; she knew Pluto always was. Back when Pluto used to constantly play Angry Birds, she and Meredith would pretend they were shooting the birds across the store, knocking down pizzas and customers instead of blocks and pigs. Another summer they climbed over the booths and the counter and snuck into the kitchen, behind the sauce and flour containers, trying to catch Pokémon.

She doubted Donna would allow them the freedom to

do anything like that now, even if Pluto wanted to. Even if Meredith wanted to. But Meredith didn't text Pluto anymore, and Pluto didn't blame her. Maybe they were too old to do that kind of stuff, anyway.

"Hey, Shooting Star." Her mom stepped over the threshold of Pluto's room and climbed into the bed with her. "I've got an idea, if you're up for it."

Pluto burrowed her face into her mom's chest, and she felt her body tense, ready for the fight. "I'm not going to the pizzeria today. You've made me go all week."

"I know, I know," her mom said. "But, I was thinking about your list and the promise you made to me, and I think today would be a good day to meet your therapist. What do you say? I made an appointment for later this afternoon, if you'd like to try for me."

Pluto looked up into her mom's big, hopeful eyes. "You don't have to go to the boardwalk?"

Her mom shook her head. "Donna's got it covered, which is exactly why I hired her. We don't even need to stop by."

Pluto considered it. She had written that list weeks ago, and she was no closer to proving to her mom she could beat this. Visiting her therapist seemed . . . doable, when even texting her dad or Fallon back didn't. "Okay," Pluto said.

"Oh, good." Her mom smiled.

It was a smile that made Pluto know she couldn't take the agreement back, even though her entire body was fighting her to do so.

Pluto did not have a panic attack in the waiting room. Her hands were clammy as she gripped the sides of the uncomfortable chair, and the sounds from the soap opera playing on the TV hung in the corner of the room put her on edge, but she did not have a panic attack. Her breathing was even, her mom's hand was gentle and soothing on her arm.

She did not have a panic attack.

Even though she felt like she might for the entire twenty minutes they waited.

Months ago—after Pluto's mom had begged and begged and even tried to pull Pluto out of her bed to make her go to school—Pluto had one of her worst panic attacks. It took over an hour for her mom to get her to breathe calmly, and when she finally did, her mom didn't mention school again. She'd called for a sitter and left for work, and Pluto went back to bed.

Her chest had hurt for the rest of the day, and she was afraid she would suddenly be unable to breathe again.

After the panic attack, Pluto called the Hayden Planetarium Astronomy Question and Answer Hotline.

She asked, "Do you know if people born with the Cancer constellation sign have panic attacks a lot?"

The voice on the other end of the line said that they didn't know all that much about zodiacs, but did Pluto want to know more about the constellation?

Pluto did not, but let them tell her about it anyway.

(The voice told her that Cancer was the dimmest out of all thirteen zodiac constellations, which was when Pluto hung up the phone.)

"Anna and Pluto Timoney?" the receptionist called, startling Pluto out of her thoughts. There was a question in the receptionist's voice and her eyebrow was slightly raised. It was the sound and look that Pluto got most often from new teachers taking attendance, the one that said, "This can't be right, can it?"

Pluto sheepishly smiled in the way she always did, that said, "Yes, that's right, that's me, that's really my name."

Pluto reached a clammy hand to hold on to her mom's.

"Hey," her mom said, bumping her shoulder into Pluto's in that way that Pluto used to love, but lately just screamed, *Get a move on.* "This is for you, Plu. You can talk to her about whatever you want, even with me in there with you. This has nothing to do with me, okay?"

I'm only here for you, Pluto thought. She nodded anyway and looked back at the receptionist.

"Ready?" the receptionist asked.

Pluto wondered if she really had a choice.

The receptionist led them down the hall to a door with a plaque that read DR. CYNTHIA COLLINS. She knocked, two small knocks with her knuckle, and opened the door. To Pluto's surprise, the room was bright. Bright blue walls, bright red couch, bright yellow lamps. It didn't match, but also it did in a way that Pluto really liked, clashing colors coming together to make something that shouldn't work, work. "Hi, Mrs. Timoney," a voice said, and Pluto stopped looking around the room to focus, instead, on the woman who was standing up from behind her desk, crossing to shake her mom's hand. "I'm Dr. Collins."

"Oh! It's Ms. Not Mrs. God, no. No. I mean, hi, hello." Pluto's mom's voice was high-pitched and weird. Pluto shot her a look. "Sorry. I think I'm nervous."

Dr. Collins's smile was kind. "That's perfectly normal. For you, too," she said, looking at Pluto. "You must be Pluto. Why don't you two have a seat and we can chat a bit? Sound good?"

Pluto turned in time to see the receptionist smile at her before exiting behind the closing door.

Pluto couldn't get her feet to move, even though her mom had already crossed the room and taken a seat on the red couch. Her mom patted the spot beside her, but still, Pluto couldn't follow.

"That's okay, you can sit when you're ready," Dr. Collins said. She was a large woman with big bones and a large mouth, and thick brown curls that seemed to float around her head. Her glasses were thin and sat low on her nose. She constantly ran a hand through her hair, giving it a messy look that didn't match the rest of her professional attire—or the formal diplomas on the walls.

Lower along the walls were bookshelves filled with children's books, and Pluto wondered if there were any about astronomy, and if there were, had she and her mom already read them? On the coffee table in front of the bright red couch were boxes filled with string and beads; a half-made necklace dangled from one.

Pluto could not breathe right.

She felt dim; she felt weighted down.

She felt like she might panic.

"Come sit, Plu. We're just going to get to know each other a bit," her mom said.

"You don't look like you want to be here, Pluto," Dr. Collins said, and Pluto wanted to say, *Of course I don't!* But she couldn't bring herself to do it.

"It's okay if you don't," Dr. Collins continued.

That didn't seem right. That didn't seem true.

"Anna, why don't you tell me a little bit about why you two are here?"

"Pluto was recently diagnosed with depression and general anxiety disorder. It got really bad about a month ago. Before that she was, well, mostly just really lethargic? Kind of moody?"

"I don't want to be here," Pluto interrupted. She took a deep, stuttering breath. "I'd like to go home now."

"Pluto, wait—" her mom started to say, but Pluto shook her head.

"You said it was okay if I didn't want to be here," she said to Dr. Collins. "I don't want to be here. I want to go home. Please."

"Shooting Star—"

"*Please.*"

"Okay," Dr. Collins said, her voice soft, her eyes kind. "Pluto, would it be okay if you waited outside the room for a minute? Can I just have a few seconds to chat with your mom before you leave?"

"But I can leave? I can go?"

"Yes." Dr. Collins nodded. "You can go."

They didn't talk about it. Her mom patted Pluto on the thigh in the car on the way home, said a supportive, "We'll try again next time," and left it at that. Pluto didn't think this was something she would be able to check off her list, because she'd failed, but she didn't want to bring it up and didn't want her mom to bring it up either.

So they barely spoke for the rest of the day.

The Mars Observer was launched into space in 1992. It was supposed to track Mars's terrain and climate. Instead, three days before it was supposed to enter Mars's orbit, its communication system suddenly stopped. Whether it was, to this day, still orbiting Mars or whether it had blown right past it into uncharted space, no one knew. It was a failure, and an embarrassment.

Therapy felt kind of like that.

Pluto Jean Timoney was due to land on Dr. Collins's couch this afternoon, but instead, she hovered by the door before disappearing back out of it, opting to orbit elsewhere.

That night, Pluto couldn't sleep. She held her wrinkled list in her hand, focused on her failed therapy visit, on her last failed attempt to have lunch with her friends, and on the planetarium visit that she was supposed to take with her mom on Pluto's birthday, which was only a couple of weeks away.

She put the list aside and started counting the chips in the paint on her walls where the glow-in-the-dark stars used to hang. She counted them a lot, when she couldn't sleep.

There were over two hundred billion stars in the galaxy. There were over two hundred billion known galaxies in space. There used to be thirty-two stars on Pluto's bedroom wall.

She started counting them again, making it to seventeen paint chips before she heard it: a gasping, sort of muffled sound that caught her ear. She rolled over to face the open threshold where her door used to be, tracing the sound down the hall in the direction of her mom's bedroom.

Pluto climbed out of bed and softly padded down the hall, wooden floor cold under her feet, with the scratch of beach sand that no matter how much her mom vacuumed never seemed to completely go away. Her mom's bedroom door (it had one) was cracked open like always, just in case Pluto needed her.

Her mom was crying. The realization of it brought a lump into Pluto's throat as she slowly pushed open the door.

Her mom was curled into her side of the bed (she always took the right side, even though she hadn't had anyone share her bed, besides occasionally Pluto, for as long as Pluto was alive), and her blond hair was draped over her hands as they covered her face. Her shoulders shook with each muffled sob, her face pressed into her pillow.

"Momma?" Pluto said, her voice rough and scratchy, as if she were the one who had been crying.

Her mom quickly sat up, eyes wide, looking as though she'd been caught stealing, finding herself in a situation she so clearly did not want Pluto to see. She opened her mouth to say something, but hiccupped a sob instead, covering her mouth with one hand and holding her other out for Pluto.

Pluto ran to her, climbing into the bed as her mom pulled her close, wrapping her arms so tight, almost too tight, around Pluto and crying into her hair. "I'm sorry, I'm sorry," her mom said, a broken whisper, even though Pluto wasn't entirely sure what she was apologizing for. Pluto just let her hold her, not knowing what else she could do, as her mom tried to stop crying, breathing deeply through her nose and noisily out her mouth. Pluto wanted to tell her, "I feel like that all the time, like I can't stop, like I can't calm down," but she said nothing.

Her mom did calm down. And with one more deep breath, she opened her eyes and looked at Pluto and smiled, a wobbly one that wasn't very convincing.

"I should know how to make this better," her mom said.

"I'll talk to Dr. Collins next time," Pluto quickly replied. "About whatever you want. I promise."

Her mom didn't respond, just buried her face back in Pluto's hair and held on tighter.

9

Two days later, Pluto was standing outside another stranger's door, her mom's grip on her shoulders almost too tight as she rang the doorbell.

A woman older than Pluto's mom opened the door, a smile on her face that made way for the deep laugh lines on her face. "Hi," she said, her curly blond hair static-clinging to the wooden frame of the doorway. "I'm Mrs. McAuliffe. You must be Pluto."

"Yep! This is Plu. Thanks for agreeing to this on such short notice," Pluto's mom was saying, and Mrs. McAuliffe responded, and her mom said something else, but Pluto missed all of it.

Because Pluto was hung up on the fact that her name was Mrs. McAuliffe. Just like the teacher from the *Challenger*.

Pluto's tutor, Pluto's teacher, was Mrs. McAuliffe.

She looked at her mom to see if she noticed, but she was still talking.

McAuliffe! It had to be a sign. It had to be.

"Hey, Shooting Star. Aren't you gonna say something?" her mom attempted to tease with a tight smile, pulling Pluto's focus.

"What's your first name?" Pluto blurted out, which definitely wasn't what she was supposed to say based on the way her mom's eyebrows shot up.

Mrs. McAuliffe laughed, and waved Pluto's mom's concern away. "Come on in, you two. Let's get to work, shall we?"

Pluto really wanted Mrs. McAuliffe to come to *their* house, had practically begged her mom to make it happen, but this was easier for Mrs. McAuliffe—at least that's what Pluto's mom had said—and, anyway, Mrs. McAuliffe was doing them a favor, since it was such short notice. (Plus, Pluto's mom hadn't worked out exactly how to pay her yet, which Pluto had learned from eavesdropping on her mom's side of a phone conversation with her dad.)

So here we observe Mrs. McAuliffe in her natural habitat.

Based on the double sets of plates on the table, the double mugs on the coffee table, and the double pairs of running shoes by the front door, she does not live alone.

No one else seemed to be home, though.

Mrs. McAuliffe was more than just a tutor, which is why she was recommended to Pluto's mom. She had a degree in psychology and experience as a counselor and therapist, and, well, Pluto should have assumed she wouldn't get a regular tutor, since she was no longer a regular kid. "Did you read that book I emailed you about?"

Pluto didn't realize the question was asked to her, and not her mom, even though she should have. Both adults stared at her, waiting for an answer. Pluto felt her cheeks grow warm. "Oh. Um."

"Answer me truthfully," Mrs. McAuliffe said. "Did you try?"

Pluto started to nod, but then stopped. "A little."

"She's been having some trouble focusing," Pluto's mom supplied, her voice quiet in the even quieter house.

Mrs. McAuliffe's smile was kind, just like Pluto's therapist's. Pluto wanted to ask her if she knew about the *Challenger*, if she knew she had the same last name as the teacher who'd been chosen for the mission, if she knew anything about astronomy. Instead, when she opened her mouth, she said: "I'm sorry."

"Don't apologize, Pluto," Mrs. McAuliffe said. "That'll just give us a place to start."

Pluto's head was swimming when they got back to the pizzeria, swirling with homework assignments, and facts about the *Challenger*, and thoughts about how cool it would be if she could go back in time and her tutor could actually be *the* Christa McAuliffe.

(There were a lot of theories about time travel, and its relation to movement through space. Pluto once listened to ten entire podcast episodes that discussed theories on traveling faster than the speed of light, and how it could create a wormhole between different timelines. Pluto didn't understand it all that much, but it was fun to think about, anyway.)

The bell above the door jingled as they entered, and the air-conditioning felt good on Pluto's skin, giving her goose bumps. "Hey, Donna!" her mom hollered as they entered.

Donna smiled and motioned to the two college girls, Kiera and Chloe, who were "working," but really were just dancing around the pizzeria, bouncing from table to table as they sang along with the old-school Britney Spears song playing on the sound system. "Glad you guys are here. These two have been doing this all day, driving me crazy."

"*You drive me crazy!*" Kiera scream-sang in Donna's direction.

Donna threw her hands up and Pluto's mom laughed. It was a quiet day in the pizzeria, but the few customers scattered throughout seemed amused. "Go join the girls, Plu."

Every year without fail, at least one of their summer employees would dance around in the restaurant. Last year, a girl named Summer (who was Pluto's favorite; she had really pretty freckles and the best raspy voice, and Pluto knew she'd remember Summer's name forever) would beg Pluto's mom to turn the radio up on slower days. She would reach for Pluto's and Meredith's hands, and they would dance and sing until they got so loud people started poking their heads into the pizzeria to see what the ruckus was.

Watching the girls dance around now made Pluto's chest feel tight. She didn't join them. Instead, she followed her mom behind the counter. "Hey, Mom, did you notice? My tutor's name is Mrs. McAuliffe."

Her mom was opening the register to see how the day had gone. "Uh-huh."

"Mom, her name is Mrs. McAuliffe. Like Christa

McAuliffe." Pluto's mom was still focused on the register. "Like the *Challenger*, Mom."

And then her mom's eyes snapped up, her face bright and eyes crinkling as she looked at Pluto. "Oh wow! How'd I miss that?" She winked. "Must be a sign, huh? You'll be in eighth grade no problem in the fall."

It *was* a sign. That's exactly what Pluto had thought.

"Anna, let's see your moves!" Kiera called out.

"Dancing is *so* not my thing!" Pluto's mom responded. "I skipped my senior prom for a comic convention!"

"How about you, Don—"

Donna cut her off before she could finish. "Don't even ask."

They didn't get all that busy that afternoon. It was one of those gorgeous—but exceptionally hot—summer days, so they sold more sodas and waters than actual pizza. Pluto was a little slow filling drinks—which made one customer angry, which made her mom angry at the customer, so she took over. Pluto moved to the corner, trying to stay out of the way.

After a while, everyone had either gone back to the beaches or gone home for the day and the bell on the door got a break until the evening crowd arrived for rides and games and pizza. When it did jingle, Pluto didn't bother looking up. She figured her mom or Kiera could take care of it.

But then her mom said, "Hey, Pluto, you want to take this one?" and Pluto looked up to see Meredith, skin summer-burned pink and thick black hair wet and salty from the ocean.

"Hi," Meredith said.

"Hi," Pluto replied. And then, noticing the sweat dripping down the side of Meredith's face, she realized why Meredith was there. "Oh! Water?"

Meredith nodded. "Two, if that's okay? My mom's like dying in this heat."

It was one of the perks of having a restaurant on the boardwalk on hot beach days. Meredith and Pluto often ran around the boardwalk, and sunbathed on the sand, growing hotter and hotter and more dehydrated than either of their parents would like before finally giving in and making their way up the beach, which by then felt like the Sahara, to the pizzeria where Pluto's mom would have cups of ice water waiting.

Pluto packed two cups with ice before filling them with water. She carefully handed them to Meredith.

"Thanks," Meredith said.

"Anything else?" Pluto asked.

Meredith shook her head. "Nah, I only came for the waters." She took both waters in her hands and turned toward the door. "Actually, I lied," she said, turning back around. "I really came to say hi."

"Oh," Pluto said. She smiled, a small but real one. "Hi."

"Hi," Meredith said, a smile on her face, too. "I gotta go, though. Mom's thirsty. And, well . . . Maybe I'll text you later?"

Pluto had flutters in her stomach, making it hard to speak, and quickly nodded. "Okay. Yeah."

The bell jingled as Meredith left. Pluto looked around for her mom, but she had disappeared into the kitchen. This was good, wasn't it? Maybe Meredith didn't hate her after all. Maybe they could be friends again, some-day, if Pluto completed her list and became Pluto again, if Pluto went to Meredith's party and things went back to normal.

Pluto felt . . . hopeful. Meredith didn't hate her, maybe. Her tutor was Mrs. McAuliffe, which had to be a sign, really. And, sure, maybe Pluto had messed up her therapy appointment, but she could try again, and maybe next time she could do it. Maybe.

A giant step back, but two little steps forward.

"You can go hang with your friend if you want,"

Donna said, coming over to lean against the counter next to Pluto. "We've got it covered here."

Pluto *was* feeling hopeful. Still, she didn't want to—*couldn't*—bring herself to hang with Meredith like they used to yet. "I'm okay. Thanks, though."

Donna looked like she had more to say, but then Pluto's mom came out from the kitchen, balancing three steaming extra-cheese pizza slices on paper plates. "Hey, how's it going?" she said, passing one slice to Pluto and one to Donna, then leaning on the counter right between them to take a big bite of her own. There was so much cheese, it pulled away from the pizza, stringy and long as her mom tried to chew through it.

Pluto smiled and said, "Meredith came to say hi."

"That was nice of her," Pluto's mom said, then glanced at Donna. Pluto ignored the look that passed between them, because it didn't matter.

She reached a hand into her back pocket, feeling the folded piece of paper she had there, her checklist that would prove her diagnosis wasn't her, that she was just fine. That was what mattered. She was still just Pluto. She could do this.

Her mom took another big bite of pizza.

Pluto, still smiling, pulled the cheese off her own.

She could do this.

10

Meredith did text Pluto that evening. *Do you want to watch something together?*

Since their parents never let them hang out after dinner on school nights, and they'd both gotten cell phones for their tenth birthdays, they would pick a movie or TV show to stream and watch it at the same time. They'd text each other comments, and it was almost like they weren't half a town away from each other, in their pajamas, ready for bed.

Pluto could do that. She could watch something from the safety of her bed. She let Meredith pick (she chose *She-Ra*), and Meredith counted down. They didn't text much, but it was more than they had since Pluto stopped going to school. They watched four episodes together before Pluto fell asleep.

~~~

Instead of focusing on her schoolwork, Pluto was trying to figure out how to ask Meredith if they could watch a TV show over text again.

"What's your least favorite school subject?" Mrs. McAuliffe asked, pulling Pluto from her thoughts. The answer was grammar—Pluto got a lot of the rules confused—but she wondered if she should lie. Would Mrs. McAuliffe want to do her least favorite subject first, to get it over with?

They were sitting on Mrs. McAuliffe's white sofa, and Pluto found herself touching the little tufts sticking out of its rounded edges.

"My cat did that," Mrs. McAuliffe said.

Pluto hadn't realized she was watching her that closely. She wanted to ask where the cat was, but she couldn't bring herself to.

"She died last spring," Mrs. McAuliffe answered anyway. "We were thinking about getting another, but, you know, then we have to worry about having another. I loved her, that little cat, but she was a bit of a brat."

Pluto almost smiled.

"What's your favorite subject, then?" Mrs. McAuliffe asked. "Mine was always science."

"Mine, too," Pluto said, and it was like those words shook the rest of her loose and she breathed a bit more normally. "I like science, too."

Mrs. McAuliffe reached into her big tote bag to pull out the science book Pluto had used all year at school. "Then let's start there, huh?"

She flipped it open, the pages familiar. It made her think about school, and about how she and Meredith sat next to each other in science class, with Harper a row in front of them and constantly getting in trouble for turning around to chat. Was it weird for that desk, the one she sat in all year, to end up empty for thirty-four days? Did Harper still turn around to talk to Meredith? She must have. Because who else would Meredith talk to?

She hoped Meredith would want to stay up late with her again, watching TV.

"What're you thinking about?" Mrs. McAuliffe asked.

Pluto shook her head. It was too hard to explain, and she didn't really want to, anyway.

"I know a thing or two about depression, you know," Mrs. McAuliffe said. And *that* reminded Pluto that as cool as it was to have her own Mrs. McAuliffe, it wasn't the same. The real Mrs. McAuliffe would know a thing or two about space, about astronomy, and not about the very thing Pluto wanted to forget. "I know, it sucks, right? It's why I went into psychology, to try to understand it better. Because I'm sure it's extra hard for your mom to understand, but you and I both know it isn't exactly a piece of cake for you either. It's closer to rocket science, right?"

That made Pluto smile.

"I know it's a lot. And I know we have to get this work done, because the school needs to see you making progress, and so does your mom," Mrs. McAuliffe said. "But you can talk to me about other things, too. If you want. When you're ready. Okay?"

Pluto wasn't really sure it was okay.

Luckily she didn't have to answer. The front door opened, and another woman walked in. She was about Mrs. McAuliffe's age, with long brown hair and bright blue eyes. "Oh! Sorry! Hi!" she said, her smile wide.

She looked so happy, like she'd never known what sadness was. Pluto looked over at Mrs. McAuliffe, but suddenly Mrs. McAuliffe looked like straight-up happiness, too. "Hey, Sunny. This is Pluto, the student I told you about."

"Pluto," the other woman said, and held out her hand

for Pluto to shake. "I'm Sunny. It is very, very nice to meet you."

Pluto smiled as she shook her hand, because her name was Sunny, and Pluto—of all people—especially liked that.

It felt like another sign. Pluto thought, maybe, she was meant to be here.

When her phone buzzed in her pocket, Pluto quickly pulled it out, hoping it was Meredith, hoping she was repairing that friendship slowly but surely.

It wasn't Meredith, though. It was Fallon.

Are you at the boardwalk this week? Can we meet tomorrow?

Fallon told Pluto to meet in their spot. Pluto didn't realize they had a "spot." They'd only met there once before. Still, she knew to meet Fallon at the visitors booth and got there first. She put in her earbuds. She was falling behind on her podcasts anyway.

"Sorry I'm late!" Pluto nearly jumped ten feet into the air when Fallon finally arrived. "Whoa, sorry for scaring you. I had to make like thirty zeppoles for some guy right as I was trying to leave."

Pluto nodded, trying to get her heart rate back to normal. "What did you want to meet me for?"

Fallon stuck her hand down into the pocket of her long

board shorts and pulled out a folded-up paperback (a different one than last time) and piece of paper. "Well, first, I brought this book for you. I thought you might like it."

Fallon held out the book. Pluto, surprised, stared at the cover for a moment. It had robots and aliens and three kids in school uniforms on it. "*Seventh Grade vs. the Galaxy*?" Pluto read, looking up at Fallon.

Fallon nodded. "Yeah! It's about a school that's a rocket ship. Like, in space. And the author actually lives in Jersey, too. And, anyway, it made me think of you so I thought you'd like it."

Pluto reached to take it and felt the blush in her cheeks. "Thank you."

Fallon shrugged and held out the piece of paper she had in her other hand. "Anyway, I made my list."

"Oh," Pluto said, taking the list. Fallon didn't immediately let go, which confused Pluto for a moment. Fallon seemed hesitant, which didn't make sense, since this was all her idea in the first place.

Pluto unfolded the piece of paper.

FALLON'S LIST:
- Get a haircut
- Convince Mom not to make me wear a dress to Grant's wedding

There was one more item, but it was crossed off in heavy black ink, so Pluto couldn't read what it said. "What was this last one?"

Fallon tensed up in that defensive way Pluto was discovering she had, where her entire body went stiff. "Nothing. I changed my mind. Just the others."

"Getting a haircut doesn't seem like a big deal," Pluto pointed out.

"Neither does going to some birthday party," Fallon fired back.

"Well—" Pluto considered it. "Okay. But why have a list at all? There's only two things on here."

"Why do you have a list at all?"

Pluto sighed. "I just don't know why you're doing this."

"Why are *you*?"

Pluto was getting annoyed that Fallon kept answering her questions with questions. "I told you why. I have to. Or I have to live with my dad. I have to show my mom I can be *fine*."

"Well I need to show my mom I can't be. That I'm not."

That answer startled Pluto. She wasn't expecting that. She looked Fallon up and down, from her old dirty sneakers to her boy shorts to her long wild hair. She was tall and lanky and stood straight and looked alert and not sleepy and not panicky and Pluto could not see what was wrong with her.

But she supposed Meredith and her mom and everyone else couldn't see what was wrong with Pluto, either. Not until it got bad, and she lost her bedroom door, and the doctor slapped a label on her.

"Things have been weird since the doctor said I have depression. I'm on medication that only kind of helps and I make my mom sad," Pluto said quietly. "I need to go to tutoring so I can be in the eighth grade in the fall. I need to go to the planetarium to make my mom happy. And I need to go to Meredith's birthday party so she'll be my friend again. And then I'm me again. I'm a full, complete Pluto again."

Fallon listened, her eyes not wavering from Pluto's. "Sometimes—" Fallon said, and then stopped.

Pluto really wanted her to keep going. "What?" she whispered.

"Sometimes," she repeated, "I don't feel right. That my hair is too long. And my school clothes are too . . ." She drifted off, trying to find the words. "My mom picks them out. That's why I wear my brother's stupid neon shorts, because she won't buy me what I like. I want my hair short like my brothers'. And I feel . . . I just . . . I don't *like* me in a dress. My brother Grant is getting married and the rest of my brothers get to wear suits and my mom picked out this really pretty yellow dress for me, but I just . . ."

She had a hard time saying it, and Pluto understood. She had a hard time explaining the way she felt, too. "Do you feel . . . are you a boy?" Pluto asked.

"No!" Fallon snapped, and then immediately softened. "Maybe? Sometimes? But sometimes not. I don't know. I'm hoping the list can help me figure it out. Or at least make me feel more . . ."

"Make you feel like you?" Pluto asked.

Fallon exhaled. "Yeah."

A flock of seagulls flew overhead, squawking and casting Pluto and Fallon in brief shadows. They both ducked slightly, focusing on the birds as they flew away.

"Okay," Pluto said, and she meant it.

Storms were common at the Jersey Shore in summertime, sometimes even bad ones like tropical storms and hurricanes and other frightening events Pluto tried not to think too hard about. When the weather was really bad, like it currently was, with lightning and rain coming down impossibly hard, her mom decided not to even open the restaurant. She called the staff and Donna and Martin and told them all to stay home. (Donna insisted she could open, but my mom insisted she get some much-needed downtime.) Anyone who went to the boardwalk on a day like this was a fool, her mom firmly believed, and she did not feel comfortable serving those fools to begin with.

Her mom was making chicken for dinner, which always came out too dry, but Pluto didn't mind. The summers were full of greasy pizzas, and dried-out chicken was almost welcome.

Pluto reached into the pan to steal a potato as her mom's cell phone started ringing. Her mom's hands were covered in breadcrumbs and oil. "Can you see who that is?" she asked.

Pluto popped the potato into her mouth, which was a mistake since it was hotter than expected, and looked at her mom's phone. Her stomach flipped. "It's Dad," she said.

Her mom looked at her for a moment before she said, "You wanna get it?"

She kind of didn't. She nodded anyway and pressed the button to answer the call. "H-hello?" she said, angry at herself for the stutter. She hadn't actually *talked* to her dad in what felt like forever. They had been doing just fine texting. He'd been teaching her the ins and outs of D&D. She didn't really understand anything he explained, but it kept him engaged at least.

"Pluto Jean? That you?" her dad said. His voice was charming as always, the sound of laughter in every word, whether or not something was funny. "How's it going, little one? I was hoping to get to talk to you."

"Fine," she said, her voice small.

"Listen, I gotta talk to your mom still, but how about you come spend the weekend here with me for your birthday? I was thinking we could start a campaign, actually get you playing D&D. It's easier to explain in person, anyway," he said, and Pluto's chest grew tight. She looked frantically over at her mom, who stopped in the middle of checking on the chicken in the oven and mouthed, "What's wrong?"

"I'm going to the planetarium," Pluto said. "With mom. For my birthday."

"I know you usually do that, but I was hoping you'd maybe want to try doing this with me this time, instead," he said. "I was thinking you could come up on Friday night, and then we'd get you home by dinner Sunday. It'll be good for you to spend some time here. Check the area out, see what it's like."

"I have a therapist here," Pluto found herself telling him. She heard her mom slam the oven door shut. "And a tutor."

"I know, I know. Just think about it, for the weekend, okay?" he continued. "You do the space thing with your mom all the time. We can go out somewhere fancy for your birthday dinner. You'd love it—"

Suddenly, the phone was being pulled from Pluto's

hand, and her mom put it to her own ear, saying, "John? It's me. You're seriously springing this on her right now?"

Her mom walked out of the kitchen, her voice doing that thing where she wanted to be whispering but also wanted to be yelling, so Pluto could hear her until she went into her bedroom and shut the door. Pluto stood in the kitchen alone, trying to get her breathing back to normal, as the chicken in the oven not only got dry, but also started to burn.

"So do you have to spend your birthday with him?" Fallon asked after Pluto told her the story.

"Mom said they made a compromise," Pluto said. "I'll stay home and go to the planetarium with her for my birthday and then go visit him the weekend after. She was really mad, though."

Fallon and Pluto sat in the pizzeria with a large pizza between them for lunch. Fallon reached for a second slice, the cheese pulling like a long string from the rest of the pie before making it, messily, into her mouth. Her eyes closed in bliss. Fallon loved pizza.

When Fallon opened her ice-blue eyes again, Pluto found herself staring into them, cheeks flushing, and was so distracted she almost missed what Fallon was saying. "Do your parents normally get along?"

Pluto almost laughed. "No, not really. Mom says they were young when they met and just grew in different directions. They used to be nicer to each other, though. They've just been fighting lately."

"My parents met when they were young, too. I'm not sure if they grew in different directions or not, but I think it was just easiest to grow together. Especially after five kids," Fallon said.

"Do you like having brothers?"

"Sometimes," Fallon said. "Grant is a lot older, so he's never really around, and Dom can be a jerk, but sometimes we play video games together. My younger brothers can be really annoying. But they're okay sometimes, too, I guess. You can come meet them if you want."

Pluto had to fight the urge to say, *No, absolutely not,* even though it sounded exhausting.

"Hey, did you read that book I gave you?" Fallon asked.

Pluto blushed again. "Not yet. My mom actually did though. I left it on the kitchen counter. She read it in like an hour; she loves sci-fi."

"I think you'll like it, too," Fallon said.

"I'm going to read it!" Pluto said, a little too loudly. "I just haven't yet. But I will. I promise."

Fallon smiled. Pluto felt herself smiling, too. She didn't know what to say next, so she didn't say anything, and the silence settled between them in a way that made Pluto feel like she *should* say something. She just didn't know what.

Luckily, her mom chose that moment to walk over. "How you two doing over here?"

"We're good!" Fallon said. "Pluto said you read the book I gave her. And that you like sci-fi? Like Star Wars and stuff?"

"Oh, no," Pluto said, preemptively rolling her eyes, knowing what her mom was about to say.

"*Trek!* I like Star *Trek*. Star Wars is great, don't get me wrong, but when it comes to science, accurate science, Star Trek at least tries to make sense and work off the real deal," her mom carried on, like she usually did when someone brought it up.

Thankfully, Fallon only laughed. "Okay. Got it."

A Lady Gaga song started playing on the radio, and since Chloe and Kiera were working the shift together again, the dancing started almost immediately. Kiera grabbed for Pluto's mom's arm, but she was having none of it. "I told you I don't dance! Accost the children instead."

So then Kiera reached for Pluto. She was about to protest, but Chloe grabbed for Fallon at the exact same time.

And suddenly, all four of them were bouncing around the pizzeria. And it felt ridiculous, and Pluto kept glancing over at Fallon to make sure she didn't think it was stupid or feel weird, but Fallon was laughing, which almost made Pluto want to laugh, too.

"That's more like it," Pluto's mom said.

The bell above the door started jingling, and Pluto turned in time to see Harper and Charlotte enter the pizzeria.

Pluto stopped dancing.

"Plu!" Harper called. "It's a million degrees outside; we were hoping you'd hook us up with some water!"

The song ended, so the girls got back to work and Fallon slid back into the corner booth, staying behind as Pluto went to meet Harper and Charlotte at the counter.

Charlotte, who had been president of their class for the past three years and was friends with everybody, noticed Fallon immediately, and she waved at her while Pluto began filling soda cups with ice. "Hi," Charlotte said.

Fallon gave her a small smile in response.

Harper pursed her lips in the way she always did right before calling out in class. "Who's that?" she asked as Pluto handed them their waters.

Fallon didn't seem to be interested in introducing herself—she was concentrating much too hard on the pizza in her hands—so Pluto said, "That's Fallon. Her family owns the funnel cake place by the arcade."

Harper exchanged glances with Charlotte.

"What?" Pluto asked, her shoulders tensing.

Harper and Charlotte exchanged glances again.

"We're meeting Meredith at the amusement park later," Charlotte said, "if you want to come hang with us."

Pluto's hands felt clammy, and the lie came easy. "I think my mom needs me here today. Donna has off on Thursdays."

"Hey, girls!" As if on cue, Pluto's mom came over and wrapped an arm around Pluto's shoulders. Pluto tensed up even more at the touch. "You guys need anything to eat?"

Charlotte shook her head. "No thanks, Ms. Timoney."

"We were just dying of thirst," Harper supplied.

Pluto's mom laughed. "Well, I'm glad I can keep you hydrated."

"We were just telling Pluto we're all hanging on the boardwalk later," Harper said, looking back at Fallon for a moment. "We asked her to come, but she said she needs to stay here?"

Pluto held her breath, because *of course* her mom was going to say that she didn't have to stay here, that *of course* she should take a break and go be with her friends, whom she hadn't spent time with in forever.

But her mom surprised her. "Actually, Harper, I do need Plu here today. But hopefully she can join you guys for a beach day soon, okay?"

Harper shrugged, and Charlotte thanked Pluto's mom a second time for the water. As they left, Pluto turned to her mom, who still had an arm wrapped tight around her shoulders.

"Thanks, Mom," Pluto said.

The smile her mom gave her was strained.

"Wake up, Shooting Star." Her mom's voice and the strands of her blond hair tickled Pluto's ear. "It's my favorite day of the year."

Pluto blinked open her eyes. Her mom was kneeling next to her bed, and the first thing Pluto saw was the burning candle, sticking out from a blueberry muffin. Pluto smiled.

"Blow it out, Plu. Let's start your birthday with a wish."

"What should I wish for?" Pluto asked, her voice barely above a whisper. It seemed super early to be celebrating.

"Oh, I can't tell you that," her mom said.

"Well, what would *you* wish for?"

Her mom made a show of thinking about it. "A year's worth of mortgage payments? No, wait. An entire year of the restaurant making more money than it loses. Oh! A huge chocolate cake, and a trip to the moon. Come on, your turn. But don't tell me what it is."

Pluto closed her eyes and really thought about it. What did she wish for? Thirteen seemed like an opportunity for a fresh start from the bad ending of twelve. An entire new year to be a new, better Pluto.

And then it came to her.

I want the International Astronomical Union to decide they were wrong. I want them to make Pluto a planet again.

She blew out the candle.

The Liberty Science Center was only an hour away in Jersey City, and every year on her birthday, Pluto and her mom saved the planetarium for last. Her mom could give better tours than the tour guides, and the way her face lit up made Pluto want to know more and more and more.

So she couldn't explain, as they pulled into the parking lot, why her heart felt like it was pounding out of her body, or why her chest was almost too tight to breathe.

She wiped her sleeve across her sweaty forehead, wiped her damp palms on her shorts. It was a hot day, but the car had air-conditioning.

Pluto realized, startled by the thought, that she wanted to go home.

The first time they went was when Pluto turned five. She couldn't remember much, but she did remember that it wasn't long after Poppy had died. Her mom had been so sad. Pluto had been sad, too, but her mom was also busy dealing with the things that need to be dealt with when someone dies, as well as dealing with the fact that she was now the sole owner of Timoney's Pizzeria.

It had been her mom's idea to go, because, she said, "We need to get out of this pizzeria and do something fun!" Pluto remembered seeing the dome of the planetarium for the first time, dark and wide and high. She remembered sitting in her mom's lap, looking up, and grabbing her mom's hands as the lights went out.

And she remembered the lights coming back on—not the ones they had just turned off, but the stars. Pluto was mesmerized by the vast darkness of outer space, beautifully illuminated by the suns and moons, planets and stars, that shot across the dome. Whoopi Goldberg's voice filled that dome, filled Pluto's head on their journey through the stars.

There, at five, in her mom's lap and wrapped up in her mom's arms, she so easily got lost in it all. Got lost in the colors of the sky and in her mother's whispers. "That's Pluto," she said, pointing. "That's you."

She'd felt like they were there, out in the universe, and she was the real Pluto orbiting, orbiting, orbiting, her mom's arms keeping her safe, both of them smiling real smiles for the first time in weeks.

Pluto took a deep breath as her mom turned off the ignition. The car instantly grew stuffier. "Mom?" Pluto said, voice shaky.

"You ready?" her mom asked, smile wide, and real, and not even a little strained, just like that first trip. Her mom loved this. Her mom loved this and loved the pre-diagnosis Pluto, five-year-old Pluto, turning-twelve-years-old Pluto. Astronomy was her everything, and then Pluto came along, and Pluto became her everything, too. Her mom shared her love of science, of outer space, of the planets and moons and stars. It was special to her, and it was supposed to be special to Pluto, too.

Mercury, Venus, Earth, and Mars . . .

Pluto had to do this. She had to do this for her list, and she had to do this for her mom.

"Yeah," Pluto lied. "I'm ready."

The Liberty Science Center, from the outside, looked

like any other gray building, except for the large sphere of the planetarium on the side. The inside, though, was magnificent. Bright blue and orange lights illuminated different areas, leading the groups of kids and adults past security and welcome booths to the exhibitions. There was the reptile house (her mom hated snakes) and the bodies exhibit full of skeletons and organs that always fascinated Meredith. (Neither Pluto nor her mom brought up the fact that ever since Pluto and Meredith had become best friends, Meredith had tagged along for Pluto's birthday. Pluto was relieved that her mom didn't ask, but thinking about it made her stomach hurt. Especially since Meredith hadn't even texted *Happy birthday!* yet.)

On the other side was the Touch Tunnel, which she and her mom always went through, even though they both hated the dark and the unknown and they released deep breaths when they came out on the other side. Then there was the Tesla show, where coils produced bursts of lightning to music, which had helped Pluto get over her fear of thunderstorms when she turned seven; and the Infinity Climber, which she was never afraid of. Pluto had been riding the roller coasters at the boardwalk ever since she was tall enough. The multistory Infinity Climber went as high as thirty-five feet above the atrium floor, and she used to climb to the top, higher than Meredith. She used to climb higher and faster and was once braver than Meredith. It never fazed her.

It fazed her now. As did the crowds and the lights and the bursts of noise that sang of science. The loud sounds of children, of animals, of lightning strikes and security guards—it was too much. She didn't want to go through the Touch Tunnel, didn't want to climb the Infinity Climber. She didn't want to see the snakes or the spiders or monkeys. She didn't want the lights of the Tesla coils and she did not want to look at dead bodies or living organisms or any of it.

She wanted to go home. She *couldn't* go home. She had to do this for her list. For her mom.

"It's crowded today," her mom observed.

The only living things known to survive in space were microorganisms, things you could see only under a microscope, like tardigrades. Meredith thought tardigrades were adorable little water bears, and Pluto thought they were actually more alien-looking than mammal—but she still wished that the Liberty Science Center was crowded with only tardigrades, not people. Maybe then she'd be able to breathe better.

Pluto hadn't brought her headphones, couldn't drown out the noise with a podcast. She tried creating one in her head instead. *Here, at the Liberty Science Center, Pluto, just like an active particle, must take up energy from her environment, must absorb the enthusiasm of the crowd around her, and convert it into direct motion to move forward.*

Her mom took her hand and frowned. Pluto's palm was warm and damp.

"Hey, Shooting Star, how about we change things up and go to the planetarium first this time. Okay?"

Pluto nodded eagerly. The planetarium was dark and calm, and she could sit next to her mom and watch the space show, and everything around her could fade away.

Her mom bought tickets to *Dark Universe* and chatted with the woman who sold the tickets while they waited to be let inside. When the doors opened, most kids and families went straight for the center, straight for the front view. Pluto and her mom knew better, knew that the best seats were the ones in the back, where you could see every inch of that dome without straining your neck, engulfing yourself in the stars.

The lights went down, and her mom leaned over to whisper, "I love it here."

Pluto wanted to respond. She wanted to agree. She wanted to mouth the words along with the Neil deGrasse Tyson narration that went along with the show they had chosen. *Way out here, ten million light-years from planet Earth, every point of light is a galaxy containing billions of stars.*

Pluto tried to relax in her seat as the room went dark and then the stars lit it back up again. *This is Neil deGrasse Tyson, and I'm here to guide you through a century of discovery about the past, present, and future of our universe.*

Pluto started thinking about her bedroom.

She used to fall asleep with the glow of her plastic stars reminding her of this moment, of each year at this very place with her mom. They'd made her feel safe, and loved, and now they were gone, and so was that feeling Pluto used to get *here*, in this planetarium.

There's no center to the universe . . . Wherever you are, it looks as if you're at the center and everyone else is speeding away.

Pluto didn't want to be here.

She *did not* want to be here.

"Mercury, Venus, Earth, and Mars . . ."

"What's that, Plu?" her mom whispered, leaning over. Pluto didn't realize she'd spoken out loud.

"Mercury, Venus . . . Mercury . . ."

She couldn't do this. She *couldn't.*

She couldn't be here, and she couldn't breathe, *she could not breathe.* She looked at her mom, who was looking up at the stars, smiling, eyes bright in the dimmed room, and Pluto knew she had to hold it together. She couldn't let her mom know she was panicking. She couldn't let her mom realize she couldn't do this. *These are the nine planets that we know. Round and round the sun they go.*

Pluto needed to fake it. She needed to hold the arms of the seat and keep her head pointed up at the stars and stay completely still. She needed to keep herself from shaking. She needed to take a deep breath and hold it. She needed to clench her teeth together. She needed to ignore the ringing in her ears. She needed to make her mom think she was okay.

When astronauts go to outer space and experience zero gravity for the first time, their bodies change. They grow an inch or two because body fluids move toward their head, which means they also get really bad headaches at first. A lot of astronauts get nauseous. And to make it even more complicated, they have to convince their body that up is wherever they point their head—even if it seems like their head is actually facing down.

That was what Pluto needed to do. She had to convince her body where up was, she had to convince her lungs they could breathe, convince herself she was fine.

When the lights came up, Pluto shrank back in her seat, blinking at the sudden bright assault. She hadn't realized the show was over. Her shoulders were tense, her jaw clenched, and she felt a little sore.

"What'd you think, Shooting Star?"

Pluto wiped her hair, damp from sweat, away from her forehead. She nodded through the ache in her neck. "Yeah. Yeah, it was great. I loved it."

By the time they got home, Pluto was stiff and sore and tired. She felt like she was coming down with a fever, even though she knew she wasn't really sick. She went straight to her bedroom and slept through the rest of her birthday.

The following morning, she didn't want to get out of bed. Her head was foggy, her body heavy. It had been a few weeks since she'd had one of these days. She wished it didn't feel like such a warm, welcome embrace. She covered her head with her blanket, trying to maintain the darkness, and waited anxiously for her mom to try to wake her.

But her mom never did. She left Pluto alone, even though Pluto could hear her go about her business through the house, knew that she was home and awake and *getting a move on*. Which was exactly what Pluto wanted, but it was also not what Pluto wanted at all.

When she finally managed to climb out of bed, she reached for her cell phone and saw how late it was, the bright light from the screen illuminating the bedroom like the stars from the planetarium.

Her dad had texted. He was excited she was coming to visit soon, and looking forward to celebrating her birthday then. Fallon had texted, too: *Happy birthday!!!* with both a cake and rocket ship emoji. Charlotte—who texted everyone on their birthdays, regardless of whether or not she was close friends with them—also sent Pluto a text.

Meredith hadn't texted. Pluto had thought they were getting back to something next to normal when they'd watched TV together, texting like they used to, but she guessed not.

The light was on in the living room, and Pluto followed it to see her mom fast asleep on the sofa, glow from the TV dancing across her face. Pluto reached for the remote to turn the TV off, and the sudden silence startled her mom awake.

For a moment, they just stared at each other. And then her mom was sitting up, rubbing her eyebrows and taking a deep breath. "Hi," she said. Her voice was rough and scratchy, and she cleared her throat before adding, "You're awake."

"Hi," Pluto said. Her voice wasn't any better.

"Guess you can check the planetarium off your list, huh?"

She wanted to say, *Can I really? Was it actually a success? Because it felt like a failure.* She wanted to know if she'd ever be able to visit the Liberty Science Center again without thinking about this birthday. She wanted to ask what her mom did when she'd turned thirteen, if it was the best birthday ever, or if she wished she hadn't had a birthday at all, wished she could never have another birthday again, wished that she would just stop getting older, stop growing, just *stop*.

Instead, she said, "Did you know that Cancer is the dimmest zodiac constellation?"

"I have something for you," her mom said, ignoring Pluto's comment and sounding so eager it made her stomach hurt.

She waited for Pluto to respond, so Pluto nodded, and her mom took Pluto's sweaty hand and led her into the kitchen.

On the table was a chocolate-frosted cake—Pluto's favorite. Her mom had made it (from a box) and stuck in fourteen mismatched candles (one was for good luck), and in red frosting she'd written, *Happy Birthday, Shooting Star.* But she'd run out of room and the last two letters of *Star* sat below the rest of them. "Did I ever tell you that I almost named you after my mom?"

Pluto shook her head. As far as she knew, she was always destined to be Pluto.

"I was so scared when I was pregnant with you. I was

young, and your dad and I were already in a weird place. My friends were off at college and partying and doing all the things young adults do. My mom was the only person I felt I could turn to, you know?" Pluto's mom paused, taking a deep breath as she blinked back the tears that shone in her eyes. "She was all I had, before I had you. My best friend."

"You miss her," Pluto said.

"All the time," her mom agreed. "But you remind me so much of her. In more ways than I can talk about right now, because it still hurts so much to talk about. But she would have been able to understand you, Plu. She'd have known what to do."

Pluto wanted to ask what her mom meant. She wanted to ask her mom about the memory she had of Poppy telling her that her grandma used to have temper tantrums, too. But her mom wiped her cheek before the tear could spill all the way down, and it struck Pluto just how *lonely* she seemed.

Pluto could relate. "Thanks, Mom." She didn't know what, exactly, she was thanking her for. She just knew that she had the overwhelming urge to say it.

Her mom smiled, and reached over to open a drawer to pull out matches.

"It's not my birthday anymore," Pluto quickly

interrupted. "And I made a wish yesterday. I don't get another one."

"Screw it," her mom said. "My house, my cake, my rules. You deserve the wish, Pluto."

Her mom started lighting the candles. Pluto noticed the slight shake in her hand, flame flickering and dancing with the movement.

She lit all fourteen and looked to Pluto.

Pluto kept her eyes on the cake, on the candles, on the flames, not wanting to see her mom's face, not wanting to see the expression in her eyes.

Still, she could not make a wish. "Will you . . . ?"

"What?" her mom asked a little too quickly.

Pluto still did not look at her. "Will you blow them out with me?"

"Yes," her mom said. "*Yes*. Ready?"

Pluto nodded.

"Three, two, one . . ."

Together, they blew out the candles. As the flames went out, Pluto couldn't help wondering what her mom was wishing for, what her mom wanted more than anything, what her mom would think if she knew how terrified Pluto was of ever going to a planetarium again.

CRITERION #2

A PLANET MUST HAVE
ENOUGH GRAVITY
TO PULL ITSELF INTO
THE PERFECT
SPHERICAL SHAPE.

Sometimes, Pluto spent all of her tutoring sessions pretending she had been sucked through a wormhole, through time and space, and was getting actual lessons from Christa McAuliffe before the *Challenger* accident could happen. It made the sessions a little more bearable, to be lost in her head, to pretend.

The real Christa McAuliffe had been chosen to go on the *Challenger* to give school lessons from space. Pluto knew she'd been chosen because of her "infectious enthusiasm," and while Pluto sat with her Mrs. McAuliffe, she found herself smiling more than usual. Her Mrs. McAuliffe had infectious enthusiasm, too, even when it came to something as mundane as math.

Pluto surprised both her mom and herself by eagerly getting ready that morning to head to tutoring.

"Can we do astronomy for my science section?" Pluto asked, in the middle of Mrs. McAuliffe's showing her how to solve for both x and y.

Mrs. McAuliffe laughed. "I think you know enough about space, Plu."

"What do *you* know about space?"

"I know enough." She tapped on the science textbook that was placed aside on the stack for later. "I also know that your seventh-grade work is all about the environment right here on Earth."

Pluto shrugged. "Earth's a planet."

Mrs. McAuliffe smiled, a big smile that seemed like it was just for Pluto. "I guess that is very, very true."

After tutoring, Pluto didn't even argue against going with her mom to the pizzeria for the afternoon, even though Donna was already there and working. It was a rare Jersey summer day where the humidity didn't make breathing feel like death and the heat feel thicker than wool, which was a nice change.

Pluto was still feeling good from her morning session with Mrs. McAuliffe, and really, she hadn't felt that good in a while. She wanted to feel the sunshine on her face. She wanted to try, finally, to enjoy the summer weather.

The college girls were dancing, Donna was in a seemingly good mood, since she didn't ask them to stop, and Pluto's mom even had a little bounce in her step as she made her way into the kitchen. Pluto didn't feel much like dancing, but still she smiled as she sat at the counter, and didn't argue when Donna asked her to "make yourself useful and wipe down the menus, they're filthy."

Pluto was about two-thirds of the way through the menus when Julie, one of the managers from Barb's Burritos next door, came through the front door, the little bell jingling. "Anna! Glad I caught both you and Donna!" she said, making her way over and leaning against the counter next to Pluto. "Hey, Pluto, it's been a while! You and your friends need to come by sometime. I'll hook you up with some quesadillas."

Pluto just smiled, and Donna hip-checked the cash register closed before saying, "What brings you by? Slow day next door?"

"You're not stealing our customers, if that's what you're implying." Julie winked at Pluto, which made Pluto's cheeks warm. "Kelly sent out a group text, I wasn't sure if you saw? They're hosting a paint night again tomor-row night. You guys need to come, we had a blast last time."

Donna wrapped an arm around Pluto's mom. "Convince this one to go, and I'm in."

Pluto saw as her mom glanced too quickly in her direc-tion, saw her mom pretend she didn't look over at Pluto at all before answering, "I really shouldn't. But you guys have fun! Send me pictures!"

Donna and Julie exchanged a look. The mood in the pizzeria seemed to change, too. The radio was playing a slow song and the college girls were actually working qui-etly, clearing tables, the dancing replaced with quick steps and *How can I help you*s and Pluto could not get out of her head the look on her mom's face as they blew out her birthday candles.

If her mom really *was* lonely, that was Pluto's fault, too.

"You should go, Mom," Pluto said. "I'm thirteen now. I can stay home alone for a couple of hours."

Her mom's headshake was small but quick. "I don't know, Pluto."

"Maybe she can have a friend over?" Donna suggested. "Safety in numbers. And they'll both have cell phones. It'll be good for you to have a night out, Anna. You live and breathe this place."

No, Pluto thought. *She lives and breathes me, like a space suit.*

"You'll just be here, Mom, on the boardwalk. I'm not a little kid anymore." Her age wasn't the issue, though. Pluto could see that, plain as day, by the concern written all over her mom's face. "I can text . . ." She was about to say Meredith, because once, Meredith would make sense. They'd spent so much time at Pluto's house or Meredith's house together that it would have made the *most* sense.

It didn't anymore, though, and Pluto took a second to think. Who made the most sense now?

"Fallon," Pluto said. "I can go over to the funnel cake shop and ask Fallon and her parents if she can stay with me."

"It's settled then!" Julie said. "I'll see you two for wine and painting tomorrow!"

Pluto's mom still didn't look all that sure.

Pluto's mom still didn't look all that sure after Fallon's parents said yes, and Fallon was ringing their front doorbell and Pluto's mom was opening it to invite her in. Fallon's gaze took in their house, and Pluto, feeling scrutinized, felt the blush move up the back of her neck. It suddenly occurred to her that she hadn't made her bed in weeks.

123

There were dirty clothes scattered around her bedroom, along with half-empty glasses of water and medication bottles sprawled all over her desk.

Not to mention she had thirty-two paint chips on the wall in her room, and a doorframe without a door that she did not want to have to explain.

"Want to watch TV in the living room?" Pluto said, and Fallon nodded, following her to the couch, the safe space where she wouldn't have to explain much of anything.

"You two sure you'll be okay?" Pluto's mom asked. She had straightened her hair and picked out one of her nicer tops and sandals, clothes that mostly lived in the back of her closet these days.

"You look nice, Mom," Pluto said. "And we'll be *fine.* Can you just go now?"

"Text me, Shooting Star. If you need *anything.*"

"Mom, *go.*"

"Okay! Okay," her mom said, rolling her eyes. "I can't help worrying, I'm your mom, get used to it, etcetera. Fallon, keep an eye on this one. I'm entrusting her to your hands!"

"Mom!"

"You got it, Ms. Timoney!" Fallon said, laughter in her voice.

It made Pluto smile, even if her cheeks were on fire.

But her mom finally left, and Pluto and Fallon were alone. "What do you want to watch?" Pluto asked. She wondered if she should suggest *She-Ra*, since Meredith seemed to really like it, and Pluto hadn't really been watching much TV lately to know what else was good, or what Fallon might enjoy.

"Hey," Fallon said. "Can I see your room?"

Pluto's stomach sank, thinking about her broken door. "Um," she said, but Fallon was already standing, and Pluto followed her out of the living room, even though Fallon didn't know the way. It was easy to find Pluto's room, though, since their home was only one floor and her bedroom didn't have a door, so Fallon was able to look right in. Pluto braced herself for the inevitable questions.

But Fallon didn't say anything about her lack of a door, or the paint chips on the wall. She didn't look at the medication bottles on her desk. Instead, she walked right over to Pluto's bookshelf, glancing at the spines and titles of all the astronomy books she had there. Pluto watched as one of Fallon's long fingers went from book to book, and Pluto shivered, as if it were her own spine that Fallon had touched. "Did you read the book I lent you yet?" Fallon asked.

Pluto sighed, looking down at her toes. "Not yet. I want to!" she quickly added. "I really do. I've just . . . it's been hard to focus. I haven't really read much of anything lately, and . . ."

"It's okay," Fallon said. "I get it. You can keep it as long as you need to. But definitely let me know when you do."

Pluto quickly nodded. "I will. I promise."

It was a relief to hear Fallon didn't mind. Pluto used to read a lot. She had read all of the astronomy books on her bookshelf and had checked even more out of the library. She'd read a bunch of her mom's old Star Trek books, and she used to always be up to date on her school reading, too.

It was just harder lately. She couldn't explain it.

Fallon pulled one of the nonfiction Star Trek books off Pluto's shelf, the one that her mom loved that discussed all of the plausible science and physics they used in the show. Pluto watched Fallon as she opened the book. She had an eyelash on her cheek, and Pluto's fingers itched to reach out and sweep it away.

The thought of touching Fallon's face made Pluto's stomach flutter, a much different feeling than the anxiety she was used to. The flutter kept her from saying anything at all, and the eyelash stayed where it was.

Fallon's eyelashes were long and dark and they fanned over her ice-blue eyes. "Neptune," Pluto said, before she could stop herself.

"What?" Fallon asked.

Pluto, who was already sweating, felt her cheeks grow warmer. "Your eyes. The color. It's like Neptune, on the bright sides away from its dark spot. Neptune is blue because of methane gas." Pluto realized she was rambling. "Sorry."

"What color is Pluto?" Fallon asked.

"Mostly light brown," Pluto said. "Which is a lot more boring."

"Your eyes are kind of gray."

Pluto smiled. "Like Mercury."

Fallon laughed, and it made the flutters in Pluto's stomach bigger. "Can I borrow this?" she asked, holding the book up.

Pluto nodded.

They sat in Pluto's room, Fallon flipping through the Star Trek book while Pluto played one of her astronomy podcasts. They weren't really talking to each other, but it didn't seem to matter. Not in the way it started to matter that last month of school, when Pluto didn't know what to say to Meredith, and Meredith couldn't understand why. This felt . . . normal. Like it used to when she and Meredith would play a video game, and they wouldn't even need to talk, both lost in their own worlds and the game play, because that was the kind of friends they used to be.

Her mom texted to check in, because of course she did, and the buzz of Pluto's cell phone was a jarring disruption. Pluto quickly sent a text back, because if she didn't, she knew her mom would probably rush home. *After* she'd sent the police and the fire department and maybe even Pluto's therapist and her dad, just for safety.

"My mom worries a lot about me," Pluto said. "She used to not worry so much. She used to let me run around the boardwalk with my friends, and I've even stayed at Meredith's without parents, just Meredith's older cousin there with us. But I'm . . . different now. So she's different, too, I guess."

"I'm sorry," Fallon said.

"I made her think I liked the planetarium so that I could cross something off my list. I made her think it was okay." Pluto sighed. "It wasn't okay. I think she'd be upset if I told her that, though."

"Hey, Pluto?"

"Yeah?"

Fallon grew quiet again for a minute, chewing on her bottom lip, her fingers playing with the corner of the book in her hands. "You think we could do something on my list today?"

That actually took Pluto by surprise, and she flushed

with embarrassment instead of whatever was warming her cheeks before. She'd forgotten about Fallon's list. "Oh. Okay, yeah. Well, what did you want to do?"

Fallon pulled out her list from her pocket, and it was just as wrinkled and worn as Pluto's. She pointed to the first item on it. "I want to start at the top," she said.

Pluto frowned. "Did you tell your mom you wanted to get your hair cut?"

"My mom won't let me cut it short, so we have to do it."

That was not what Pluto wanted to hear. "Wait, wait, wait. We can't just go to the hair salon ourselves. What about your dad? Or your oldest brother maybe?"

Fallon shook her head, eyes narrowing, her hands tightening on the list. "No. *No.* It has to just be us, Pluto. My mom . . . ever since we moved, she's so busy with funnel cakes and Grant's wedding, and my other brothers are just constantly everywhere getting to just . . . be *them* and I need to do something that's *me*. When Tommy was three he cut our neighbor's hair. He did it so bad, her mom had no choice but to get it cut short for real."

Pluto, eyes wide, started shaking her head. "Your brother was three! He didn't know better. I'm *thirteen*! I do! *We* do!"

Fallon's nose turned red, and Pluto really hoped she wouldn't start crying. "I need to do this," Fallon said, her voice soft.

"I know, but . . ."

"Please. *Please.* Help me do this. You said you'd help me with my list."

Fallon's face was open and begging and eager.

It reminded Pluto of her mom.

And just like she couldn't let her mom know how much she panicked during the planetarium show, she couldn't let Fallon down, either.

"Okay. I'll do it."

Pluto found scissors in one of the kitchen drawers. They were big and clunky, and kind of rusted at the edges. Pluto felt a little light-headed holding them.

Fallon took a seat at the kitchen table, reaching for the dish towel to drape around her shoulders as a makeshift smock. It made things look a little too real for Pluto, who wasn't really convinced this was a good idea.

She reached for Fallon's hair, soft and thick and curly in her hand. "Fallon, I don't know if I can do this. Your mom's going to be so mad. At *me*."

"She'll get over it," Fallon said. "She needs to get over it."

"What if she doesn't?" Pluto asked. "What if she doesn't let us hang out anymore?"

"I'll still hang with you anyway," Fallon said, as if it was the easiest thing imaginable.

But it wasn't, not to Pluto, who had a hard time talking to, let alone hanging out with, all of her old friends. Who'd barely spoken with her best friend for months. Who'd barely wanted to go anywhere, be with anyone, except her mom. Except for Fallon. She didn't know what she would do if she lost that.

She didn't know how to tell Fallon she needed her, either.

Her fingers grazed Fallon's neck, and when Fallon shivered from the touch, so did Pluto. Pluto swallowed, but didn't move her hand, as she carefully made the first cut. Long brunette strands fell gracefully, twirling down to the floor.

At the same time, the front door opened.

"Hey, you two! How was your evening? What are you—" Her mom's words got caught in her throat as she took in the sight of the two of them, both looking back at her with wide eyes, like deer in headlights. "What?

Why?" The last question was shrill and loud in the small space.

"I asked her to!" Fallon said, as Pluto's mom dropped the painting she'd made during her evening out to grab for the scissors still in Pluto's hands. She yanked them from Pluto so roughly, it hurt. "I wanted her to," Fallon added.

"You don't just . . . you're *thirteen*, not five, Pluto!" her mom yelled. Pluto couldn't remember the last time her mom had scolded her like this. In a way that felt so . . . normal. Her mom still had the scissors gripped tightly in her hands, and she ran her hand through Fallon's hair, or at least what was left of it. "Okay. Okay," her mom said, rubbing her eyebrows. "Okay, Fallon, I need to take you home. I need to—Jesus, what were you two thinking! We trusted you, *I* trusted you, on your own!"

"I'm sorry, Mom," Pluto said, even though she wasn't sure she meant it.

"I'm sorry, Ms. Timoney," Fallon said, even though Pluto *knew* she didn't mean it.

"Both of you get your shoes on and get in the car," her mom said, and Pluto nodded. Her mom hadn't yelled at her in so long, and it felt so weird, but it felt so normal and right and like *before*, that Pluto . . . liked it. Which made it all feel weirder.

Pluto sat in the back seat, her leg bouncing, as she

waited for her mom to come back after delivering Fallon to her front door. Pluto couldn't hear anything, could barely see anything except for Fallon's mom ushering them both inside. She glanced at the car clock. It had already been six entire minutes.

When her mom finally came back to the car (eleven minutes later), she looked as though she was going to start screaming all over again. Instead, she closed the door as she climbed into the driver's seat, leaned against the headrest, and sighed. "I cannot believe . . ."

"Was Fallon's mom mad?" Pluto asked.

"Was Fallon's mom *mad*?" her mom said, voice raised, before taking a deep breath and adding, more quietly, "*Furious*. She's going to have to get Fallon's hair cut so short just to fix it"—Pluto couldn't help the smile on her face, which her mom immediately noticed—"which is clearly what you wanted. Oh my God."

Pluto would ask if she was grounded, but she didn't know what her mom could possibly do to ground her. She couldn't tell Pluto to stay in her room, since she was always the one dragging Pluto out of it. She couldn't tell Pluto she wasn't allowed to see her friends, since Pluto already did that to herself.

Her mom just shook her head. "I can't believe you cut that poor kid's hair."

"She really did want me to," Pluto said.

"Yeah, well, she got her wish."

"Did you paint a pretty picture?" Pluto asked.

Her mom threw her hands up. "You know what? I did! I'm a great wine-and-paint painter apparently! Better than you are at cutting hair, at least!"

Suddenly, Pluto couldn't help the feeling that started deep in her gut and pushed tightly into her lungs. She started *laughing*, even if she knew she was in trouble, even if it made her mom spin around in her seat and stare at her as if she'd sprouted an extra head. She couldn't help it. Deep, belly laughs that she couldn't stop, because Fallon *had* gotten her wish. Fallon could check something off her list. It worked. It *worked*, and it made Fallon happy and it made Pluto happy, and if Fallon could check something off her list, Pluto could, too. She *could*.

And then her mom started laughing, too, and Pluto wasn't even sure why they were both laughing so hard together, but the sound filled the car, and it felt good, and she couldn't remember the last time they'd both found something so funny.

Her mom managed to punish Pluto anyway, by making her take out the trash at the pizzeria. She hardly ever gave Pluto this chore, since the black trash bags ended up being nearly the size of Pluto (the planet, not the person), and Pluto wasn't allowed to drag them. The last time she did, they'd caught on the splintered boardwalk, and sauce and plates and pizza crusts got all over. The seagulls had swarmed and had their own garbage party.

The planet Earth is lush and green, except for the landfills. So much garbage, so little space, and here on the Jersey Shore, seagulls cannot get enough of it!

Pluto would not be making that mistake again. So she carried the garbage bags, one at a time, to the dumpster.

When she came back inside, with gross greasy *something* dripping down her arm from a tear in one of the bags, Meredith was standing there, waiting for her.

"Oh," Pluto said. "Hi."

She hadn't heard from Meredith since they'd watched TV together. Not a single text. (In fairness, Pluto hadn't texted either, because every time she picked up the phone and looked at the send button, her heart thudded loudly in her chest and up into her throat and she was afraid that Meredith wouldn't want her to, anyway.)

Meredith didn't say anything, just shifted her weight from foot to foot, toying with the envelope in her hands. Back near the door, her older cousin Nico was waiting. Nico babysat Meredith during the days both her parents had to work, and she hated the beach (and the sun—she was very pale, with black hair streaked with pink and purple), so Pluto knew they were there for a reason, not for a beach day.

"What's up?" Pluto said after a few seconds of Meredith's saying nothing.

Meredith looked . . . angry. "My mom told me to bring you an invitation to my birthday party," she said, thrusting the envelope toward Pluto. "But you don't have to come. You probably wouldn't anyway, but I don't really want you there."

Pluto felt like she might cry. "You don't?"

"I've wanted to be your best friend for weeks and weeks, but you don't want to be mine anymore," Meredith said. "And it was okay when you were sick, but you're not sick. You look fine, and Harper said . . ."

"What did Harper say?" Pluto asked.

"You have a new best friend. She and Charlotte saw you. You won't be my friend but you'll be someone else's friend, and I don't want to be your friend anymore, Pluto."

Pluto couldn't help the tear that dripped down her cheek. Meredith had tears dripping down hers, too. "I'm sorry," Pluto said, and she meant it. She was sorry. She was sorry that she stopped being Meredith's friend, that she didn't know how to take it back, that she didn't know how to fit back in again. That it was easier with Fallon because Fallon hadn't known Pluto before the diagnosis. Fallon was different, felt different, and it wasn't the same.

Meredith wiped her cheeks. "My mom said to invite you, but you don't have to come," she said again, and turned on her heel and made her way back to Nico.

And then she was gone. Pluto didn't chase after her.

14

Take medication. Visit the planetarium with Mom. Go to Meredith's birthday party. Go to 8th grade in September. Visit therapist.

Pluto was taking her medication every morning, but really, what else had she accomplished? She'd had an unsuccessful trip to the therapist. Meredith did not want her at her birthday party. As far as her mom was concerned, Pluto could cross off the planetarium, but she didn't, not on the paper in her pocket, because how could she? And to top it all off, her dad was expecting her to visit him for the weekend, where he wanted to "show her around" and "see how she likes things there."

She was afraid her mom was going to drop her off and leave her there, where her dad could try to fix her, and her mom wouldn't have to keep dealing with the broken pieces.

Her mom was currently packing her bag. "What time will you come get me?" Pluto asked.

"Sunday? Early afternoon, probably."

"But what time?" Pluto asked.

"We'll figure it out once we get there and talk to your dad," her mom said. It wasn't good enough for Pluto, who was having trouble breathing, who just wanted a set time so she could count down the hours. *Mercury, Venus, Earth, and Mars . . .*

"Hey, it's okay. What's wrong, Plu? Let's talk about this." Her mom was kneeling on the floor of Pluto's bedroom, pulling clothes out of the dresser to pack.

Pluto's eyes drifted to the chips in the paint, counting seven before saying, "I don't want to go to Dad's."

"It's just for a couple of days. He's your dad, Plu. He loves you. You'll have a good time, okay? I promise," she said, and then shook her head. "Okay, no, I can't promise that. But he's got a whole weekend planned, and you can tell him if you're not feeling up to anything, and it'll be fine. You might surprise yourself and enjoy some time away."

"Can you just come with me?"

Her mom's laugh had no humor in it. "That's not a good idea. Your dad and me in the same room all weekend is just asking for disaster."

"I don't want to be alone," Pluto said.

Her mom stopped packing. "You'll be with your dad."

Pluto felt like she might cry, and her mom must have noticed, because she pulled Pluto close in a tight hug. It didn't make Pluto feel any better.

But then her mom pulled back, and there was an excited smile on her face. "I have an idea."

Which is how Fallon ended up buckled into the back seat with Pluto as they drove up the turnpike and through the Lincoln Tunnel, making their way to the center of New York City.

Fallon's hair was short and curly, off her neck and out of her eyes, and Pluto loved it. Fallon looked lighter, as if the weight of her hair had fallen heavily on her shoulders before and now she was free to keep her head up, for her eyes to shine and her smile to be even more visible. Or maybe she was just smiling more that day. Regardless, Pluto could not stop looking at her.

"What?" Fallon said, when she caught Pluto staring.

Her eyes narrowed in their defensive way, her cheeks turning pink. "You don't like it."

"No!" Pluto nearly shouted in the small space of the car. "I *love* it!"

Her mom smiled in the rearview mirror. "Your mom is a better person than I am, Fallon, to agree to leaving you in Pluto's care again."

Pluto rolled her eyes. Fallon laughed.

In fairness, Pluto *was* surprised Fallon's mom had agreed to let Fallon come with her for the weekend, too, but her mom had been on the phone with Fallon's mom for nearly an hour. Pluto tried not to listen, but she knew her mom had told Fallon's mom *everything*.

Which should have made Pluto feel more like a pity friend, a charity for Fallon, but really, she was just relieved. She didn't have to face the uncertainty of the city or her dad's apartment alone. And now her mom *had* to come pick them up at the end of the weekend.

They came out of the Lincoln Tunnel into what Pluto could only describe as chaos. Cars on either side of them, horns honking, tires skidding, as they wove in and out of their lanes. Crowds of people crossing at crosswalks, and before crosswalks, distracted by taking pictures and in a hurry to get to wherever they needed to be. Tall buildings stretched up and out and covered them in shadows, even though the sun was bright that day. Pluto's mom had her window rolled down and her sunglasses on as she hummed along to the radio, not noticing, or at least not caring about, the sticky heat, the smoggy wet smells, the clamor and noise and busyness.

In the second grade, Pluto made one of the most popular of science fair projects: a Styrofoam solar system, the planets circling the sun when she pushed them along their orbits. But now, Pluto knew enough about space to know that the planetary alignment of those painted balls in her science project couldn't possibly do the real thing justice. In reality, they move at different speeds, in different directions, circling at their own pace, in their own orbit.

That was what the city felt like now, as Pluto stopped looking out her window.

You don't need a telescope to find chaos in the universe—just look right outside your window.

Pluto already missed the clear view of the sky, the sound of the seagulls, the space of the boardwalk.

They pulled up alongside a building, behind a man with a Nuts4Nuts cart. Pluto's mom threw the car in park and pressed the button for the hazard lights to flash on. "Okay, let's get a move on before I get a ticket," she said.

Fallon grabbed her backpack and jumped out of the car. Pluto was not as quick to follow, but she did grab her bag and climb out, looking up at the sky. She didn't think she'd be able to see any stars here at night, wouldn't be able to point to the constellations and think of her mom. Her mom didn't belong here. This was her dad's place. He never had any use for the solar system. He was always much more concerned with what was in his mind, in the fantasies of D&D.

His concern hardly extended to Pluto, before the diagnosis. After—when she started falling asleep more in class, and turning down invitations to go to Meredith's, and getting angry at her mom, and not eating dinner, and locking herself in her bedroom as the weight in her lungs got heavier and heavier until she snapped, until her mom had to break down her door—he started calling more. He started asking about her more.

He started blaming her mom more.

And after thirteen years of truce and peace, of him with his apartment and job in the city and her mom with Pluto and the restaurant in New Jersey, things changed. They began fighting. About what was best for Pluto. About who could take care of her better.

They made their way to the front doors, and Pluto's mom stared at the intercom for a bit, at the buttons next to apartment and floor numbers. "Do you remember what your dad's apartment is?"

"1668," Pluto said. *The year Newton invented the first reflecting telescope.*

Her mom pushed the button.

The door buzzed, unlocking, and her mom pushed it open.

They took the elevator up, and Pluto kept quiet, and her mom kept quiet, so Fallon kept quiet, too. Pluto had never been to her dad's newest city apartment. He mostly came to her, when he took the time to come at all.

Pluto's dad was waiting on the other side of the elevator doors as they opened. His smile was wide, his boyish face and floppy hair making him look much younger than he was. Pluto's mom always said he looked like a little boy playing dress-up, and Pluto had to agree as he stood there in his button-up shirt and tie, arms outstretched. "There's my girl!" he said.

Pluto walked into his open arms, and he wrapped them around her tight. She held her breath until he let go. "Hey, Anna," he greeted Pluto's mom, reaching an arm out to take Pluto's bag from her. "You look good."

Her mom smiled, but it was hesitant and small. "You do, too. It's good to see you."

Pluto's dad looked over at Fallon. "You must be . . . Frankie?"

"Fallon," Fallon said. "Nice to meet you, Mr. Timoney."

Which made Pluto's dad cringe, because he was Mr. Wyle. Pluto had her mom's last name. "Just call me John," he said.

He looked back at Pluto's mom, and for a moment they all stood awkwardly in the hallway. "You'll pick her up Sunday?" he finally said. "I mean, you can come in if you want. I wasn't sure if you wanted to get going, or . . ."

"I'm double parked." Her mom rubbed her eyebrow. "I'll get them Sunday afternoon. There's going to be traffic no matter when I come, but that seems the safest option. She's got her medication in her bag, it's set up for her, just make sure she takes it with—"

"I've got it," her dad interrupted. "And I'm sure Pluto Jean knows, too."

Her mom's smile wavered. "Can we talk for a minute? Alone?"

Fallon shifted her backpack from one shoulder to the other, and Pluto didn't blame her for the way she kept her eyes down at the floor.

Pluto's dad hesitated another moment before walking over to the door in front of them, the number *1668* hung in brass at the top. He turned the knob and pushed the door open, holding it as he gestured to Pluto and Fallon. "You two go on in. Your mom and I will chat, and then we'll talk dinner, okay?"

"Let me get a hug, Plu," her mom said, and Pluto fell into her arms. Her mom held her tight, burying her face in Pluto's hair, her mom's dyed-blond strands mixing with Pluto's wheat shades. "You be good, Shooting Star. Remember what I said. I'm a phone call away. You and Fallon have fun."

Pluto nodded into her mom's shoulder.

"I'll be right in," her dad said, still holding the door, as if he, too, wanted Pluto to *get a move on*.

Pluto's dad gestured once more for her and Fallon to go inside, and this time they did. She wondered what they were going to say about her behind the closed door.

Pluto's dad said his apartment was big, and honestly, it made Pluto wonder what he considered small. She knew he thought their house in Keansburg was tiny, and being here, in his home, she didn't think that assessment was fair.

His kitchen and living room were combined to make one big room. He had one couch, a TV hung up on the wall, and a kitchen counter but no table. The counter had two barstools, but that was it, and Pluto wondered if he ate dinner there, or if he used the coffee table in front of his sofa. "My bedroom is that room back there," he said, motioning, "and the bathroom is right next to it. I've got an air mattress blown up in my office, right through here."

She looked around for photos of him and his girlfriend, or even of Pluto, but found nothing but simple artwork hung on the walls that Pluto thought might have come with the frames. Her dad's shoes were strewn by the door, and he had dirty dishes in the sink, a throw blanket bunched up on the couch, and half-drunk bottles of water on rubber coasters on his coffee table. A small Bluetooth stereo was playing jazzy classical music that Pluto remembered he loved. His apartment looked lived in but boring. It looked like he was there, but not really there.

His office was a bit cluttered, which made Pluto feel more comfortable, even if there was hardly any room for the air mattress set up on the floor with sleeping bags on top. His desk was covered with papers and his laptop, two empty coffee mugs, and a set of large multicolored dice that Pluto knew he used for playing D&D. There was a framed photo of him and a woman Pluto didn't know (Was that his girlfriend? He talked about her a little, but Pluto had no idea what she looked like), and a second one of Pluto. She was just a baby, with wisps of hair and no teeth.

There was a third photo, not framed, with a crease

down the center as if it had been folded at some point, that was leaning where his desk met the wall. Pluto didn't know most of the people in the photo—it was a group shot—but she recognized her mom and dad almost immediately. They were all dressed up, in old-timey costumes, smiles and laughter shining in their eyes.

"When was this taken?" Pluto asked.

"Maybe two years before you were born? It was at the Ren Faire upstate. We used to have so much fun at those. I haven't gone in years, though." He reached for the photo from Pluto's hands. "I know you and your mom share her love of space, but maybe if you come here, we can share something, too. Go to a Ren Faire together. Or maybe even New York Comic Con in the fall. I bet even your mom would come with us to that one."

Pluto's shoulders tensed at the thought. Both sounded exhausting. "Maybe."

"It might be nice to have something to bond over. Like you and your mom do. I don't really get a chance to do any of this stuff anymore, and even my D&D group has dwindled over the years. It would be nice to have a new buddy to do it all with again." He put the photo back on the desk. "You two get settled in, and then we'll decide what to eat for dinner, okay?"

He walked out of the office, leaving them, and Fallon dropped her backpack to the floor. "Your dad seems nice."

"My mom says he's 'charming,' " Pluto responded.

"Thanks for inviting me," Fallon said, picking up Pluto's dad's dice. "It's . . . I'm very happy to not be home. Do you think your dad will teach us how to play Dungeons & Dragons? I want to be something cool. With like, a big sword." Fallon motioned slicing the air with her imaginary weapon.

Pluto laughed. "Having to be in charge of a big sword or being responsible for any sort of adventure would make me too nervous. That's probably why my dad and I never bonded over it before."

"You like sci-fi, though. Fantasy's just another type of imagination."

"Physics and technology aren't imaginary."

Fallon rolled her eyes. "Don't tell your mom I said this, but I read that Star Trek book. I'm not too convinced any of it could be real."

Pluto's dad decided they should order takeout and, as he said, "get a fresh start tomorrow." Pluto didn't know what that meant, but she focused instead on the stack of takeout menus her dad handed her for her and Fallon to choose from. Pluto immediately vetoed pizza, and Fallon chose Chinese.

Her dad ordered, and for fifty-two minutes, they sat in silence watching old sitcom reruns on TV until the doorbell rang. "That's Sarah with the food," her dad said, jumping up to answer it.

Pluto froze as Fallon asked, "Who's Sarah?"

Sarah was her dad's girlfriend.

Her dad opened the door and leaned in to kiss Sarah before letting her inside. "Hi!" she said, entering the apartment. "I'm Sarah."

Sarah looked . . . well, if Pluto was being honest, she looked alarmingly like Pluto's mom, if Pluto's mom ironed her clothes more often and wore dresses. Their hair was the same shade of blond (Pluto was tempted to ask Sarah what her dye number was) but Sarah's was shorter, cut above her shoulders. Her eyes, though, were bluer and her smile wasn't the same.

Still, she looked friendly as she kicked off her shoes and crossed the room to join them. "Which one of you is Pluto Jean?" Only her dad ever used her full name. He hated that her mom named her Pluto. Adding her very normal middle name seemed to make him feel better.

"Me," Pluto said, but her voice was so raspy, the word barely came out at all.

Sarah sat down right next to her. She put her large blue pocketbook down on the floor and reached into it, pulling out a small bottle of hand sanitizer, squeezing out a drop, and rubbing her hands together as she spoke. "I've been looking forward to meeting you. Don't worry, I'm sticking around all weekend. If it were up to your dad, he'd keep you in here the whole time, and where's the fun in that? I thought this visit called for more of an adventure."

That made Fallon smile, but Pluto thought staying in the apartment the whole time, instead of facing the *outside* in the *city*, sounded pretty good to her.

Her dad set up plastic plates and utensils on the counter for her and Fallon, and he and Sarah ate at the coffee table. Sarah *was* friendly. She asked Fallon about her family and about the boardwalk; she half-heartedly scolded Pluto's dad when he dropped lo mein on the floor. ("For someone so organized, your dad's such a mess.") She used her hand sanitizer consistently throughout dinner, except for the time she caught Pluto watching her and she dropped it back into her bag instead.

The entire ordeal was a bit much for Pluto, who barely ate anything.

Afterward, Fallon helped Sarah pick out a movie on Netflix as Pluto excused herself to the bathroom. She paused as she passed her dad's bedroom. The door was ajar, and before she could stop herself, she pushed it open.

His bedroom had a huge window that made Pluto

gasp, and she made her way over to it, pushing back the curtain to see the city view.

It was incredible. The lights from the buildings and cars and streetlamps were bright, and Pluto felt like she could see the whole city and none of the darkness that usually came at night. She placed her hand against the glass, cool against her skin as she watched life unfold around her. Nothing stopped moving in the universe; it was constantly in motion, and that seemed so obvious in New York City.

She looked up toward the sky and saw mostly buildings. The bits of sky she did see were empty.

"Great view, huh?" her dad said, making Pluto jump. "Sorry! Didn't mean to scare you."

Pluto looked back out at the city. It kept going. There was no stopping, no stars. There was no moon, and no quiet. *Mercury, Venus, Earth, and Mars . . .*

"I'm so glad you're here," he said, wrapping an arm around her shoulders. "I think you're going to love it."

Pluto didn't think so. She didn't think someone like her belonged here.

15

Pluto woke to someone gently shaking her shoulder, Fallon's voice in her ear. "Pluto?"

Pluto pulled the scratchy sleeping bag over her face and rolled over onto her other side.

"Your dad and Sarah said we'd go get breakfast when you woke up," Fallon went on. "But it's . . . almost lunchtime, so they gave me some cereal, and said maybe we could get food later. You've been sleeping for a while."

Pluto felt like she'd hardly slept at all, and she wanted to sleep longer.

The Mars Exploration Rover requires power to move or communicate with Earth. The main source of power

153

comes from the solar panels that sprout from its sides like wings.

Pluto sometimes thought she needed sleep the way the Mars rover needed sun. After using too much energy, she needed to recharge. Until she did, Pluto could not move and could not communicate with anyone on Earth, either.

The air mattress dipped as Fallon climbed back on, lying down next to Pluto. Pluto turned to face her, and slowly blinked open her eyes. Fallon smiled. "You can sleep a little longer, if you want," she said. "I can read. I brought a book with me."

The Mars Exploration Rover had backup batteries, just in case the sun *didn't* shine. Pluto didn't have a backup, didn't have anything to give her an extra boost when she felt like she just couldn't, unless she counted her medication.

Pluto nodded. Fallon reached into her bag and pulled out a book.

She woke again an hour later, Fallon still reading next to her. Pluto felt the back of her neck grow warm. "You didn't have to stay," she said. She wished Fallon hadn't. Her dad, and Fallon, and Sarah . . . they had all weekend to see post-diagnosis Pluto. It was a lot of hours and minutes and seconds for them to realize exactly what Pluto's label meant.

The Mars Exploration Rover's batteries would

eventually stop working. There would come a day when it wouldn't be able to recharge at all.

"I didn't mind," Fallon said. "Are you okay?

"I'm tired."

"Can you get up now, though, you think?" Fallon asked, and as if on cue, her stomach grumbled. She laughed. "My stomach would appreciate it."

Pluto didn't laugh, but she did manage to smile.

They took turns washing up and dressing in the bathroom, and then found Sarah waiting on the sofa for them. She was rubbing her hands together and smiled when she saw them. "Oh good!" she said. "You're awake. You must be starving."

Pluto shrugged, but Fallon nodded.

"Your dad's just in his room on the phone with work, but once he's off, how about we go for some lunch?" Sarah said. "What do you guys think?"

"That sounds good to me!" Fallon said, before wiping her nose on her shirtsleeve.

Pluto wouldn't have noticed if it didn't seem to immediately draw Sarah's attention. Sarah paused, like she was frozen in the middle of making a decision, but then she made that decision and pulled the hand sanitizer out of her bag. She used it before motioning for Fallon to hold out her hands.

"Sorry," Fallon mumbled, rubbing the sanitizer in her palms.

"No, it's okay. Seriously, no worries," Sarah said, smiling as she dropped the sanitizer back into her bag. "There's tissues on the counter if you need, though."

Fallon reached for a tissue.

"Sorry about that," Pluto's dad said as he finally came out of his bedroom. "I can't handle it when people are incompetent. Makes me have to do double the work." He was buttoning the last few buttons on his shirt. "Let's get going."

Her dad opened the apartment door and held it for the rest of them. Fallon stepped into the hallway, and before Pluto could follow her, Sarah gently touched her shoulder. "I don't mean to overstep, but I don't think your dad's on top of things and I need to check. Did you take your medication?"

Pluto blinked, startled and annoyed, even though Sarah was right. Pluto had forgotten about the baggie of medication that was shoved deep in her travel pack. She felt her cheeks turn pink and she looked down at the floor.

"Hey, no worries," Sarah said. "I forget sometimes, too."

Pluto's eyes jerked up to meet Sarah's. She took medication too? Pluto wanted to ask about it but couldn't find the words. Did Sarah have bad days too, where she couldn't get out of bed? Did she worry so hard sometimes it made her sick? Did she get angry, and sad, and scared, without knowing why?

Was she like Pluto?

Sarah must have seen all the questions written on Pluto's face. She pulled out her little bottle of hand sanitizer, dripped some onto her hands, and began rubbing them together again. "I do this a lot," Sarah said. "I can't help it, especially now that it's in my mind since we're talking about it. It's called OCD—Obsessive Compulsive Disorder—and I need to keep my hands clean, among other things. Even if they are clean. Even if I sometimes do it too much and my skin gets dry and raw." She showed Pluto her hands, where some of the skin on her palms was red and peeling.

It wasn't the same. But it was the first time Pluto felt like someone could really understand her. "I have depression and anxiety."

Sarah smiled and said, "So go take your meds, and we'll get going."

Fallon ordered a turkey sandwich the size of her head, and Pluto got a BLT. Her dad did, too, but like the big kid her mom said he was, he got his with a side of cheese fries. Sarah got a salad topped with chicken, and let Pluto's dad pick out the cucumber slices to pop in his mouth.

Sarah used hand sanitizer four times as they ate and excused herself to the bathroom to clean her hands once she was finished. Pluto couldn't help watching her each time she pulled the little bottle out of her bag. After the third time, Sarah caught her looking and hesitated.

Pluto blushed, feeling guilty for watching. "Sorry."

"No, no, it's fine," Sarah said. "I get a little embarrassed sometimes. When it first started, I didn't even want to leave the house or tell anyone what was happening." She was still holding the sanitizer in her hand, her other palm outstretched as if someone had hit pause on her.

"I understand," Pluto said. And she did. She felt like she understood better than anyone, and she really wanted Sarah to know that. She wanted Sarah to understand *her*, too.

"So what should we do today?" Pluto's dad interrupted. He turned to Sarah. "Your niece liked that American Girl doll store, right? We could do that."

Pluto had not played with dolls since she was five, but of course her dad wouldn't know that. (She doubted Fallon ever played with dolls, by the horrified look on her face.)

"I think, with it being such a gorgeous day out, it

might be nice to head to the park for a walk," Sarah said. "Oh! We could window-shop on our way. Everyone loves window-shopping."

Pluto's dad's phone started ringing. "I'll be right back," he said. "I have to take this."

He excused himself from the table, and Pluto thought about having to go outside, into the big lively city, where nothing ever stopped, and everything was fast and loud and *moving*, and Pluto felt small and tired and . . .

"We could always go right back up to your dad's place if you don't like it," Sarah suddenly said. "We can order too much food and watch way too much TV."

Pluto turned to Fallon, who was waiting for Pluto to take the lead. Fallon, Pluto knew, would go along with anything.

So, it seemed, would Sarah.

They would do whatever Pluto wanted, whatever she needed. Which was . . . well, if Pluto was being honest, it was *awesome*. She hadn't felt this in control of anything in her life for quite some time.

"Is the park far?" Pluto asked.

Sarah shook her head. "You probably saw it from your dad's window. Just a few blocks up from here. We could walk it."

Pluto's dad came back to the table. "Okay, you girls are

going to have to fly solo today. I have to go fix something at the office; everyone there is useless. But I'll catch up with you for dinner. How's that sound?"

"John, really?" Sarah asked, brow creased. "I'm not . . . you really have to go?"

He placed a quick kiss on her cheek. "Just a couple hours. Go to the park. Shop. Have fun. You don't need me getting in the way." He turned to Pluto. "Okay, Pluto Jean?"

They all looked at her.

Pluto could say she wanted to go back to bed, and they would let her. She could ask to be left alone, and they would go along. They wouldn't push her to *get a move on* if she didn't want to.

She realized with a jolt that she *did* want to go.

"Okay," Pluto said. "Let's go to the park."

It was a surprisingly good day. Pluto liked it. She liked the city, she liked being in the city, even though it was loud and it was crowded, and she liked that when she reached for Fallon's hand, Fallon took it and held it tight the whole time.

She didn't like all of it, though. She didn't like the grates that smelled of smoke and gas and garbage, and she certainly didn't like walking over them, especially when she could hear the subway trains underneath. She didn't like looking up, up, up at the tall buildings that made her feel light-headed. She didn't like the way people rushed by and bumped into her and made her lose her hold on Fallon's hand.

But she liked the way the sun reflected off the windows of the buildings. She liked that the park seemed surrounded by those buildings.

Here in the city, hidden behind the barricade of skyscrapers, you can find isolated green grass and trees and a reservoir, the city's own little secret wilderness waiting to be explored.

The pigeons reminded Pluto of seagulls, which reminded her of home, so she liked them, too. She liked the horse-drawn carriages, the smell of Nuts4Nuts, the fancy clothes in the store windows.

Fallon liked the clothes in the windows, too, and as they walked along Fifth Avenue, Pluto only realized Fallon had slowed her pace when she gently pulled free of Pluto's hand. Fallon was staring into a store with elegant tuxes, three-piece suits with different color ties and pocket-handkerchiefs.

Pluto remembered Fallon's list, that Fallon did not want to wear a dress to her brother's wedding.

"You'd look really nice in one of those," Pluto said.

Fallon blushed, but she couldn't hide her smile.

Pluto liked making her smile.

Sarah got them ice cream, and Fallon and Pluto ate their cones as they climbed the rocks on the edges of the reservoir, looking out at the water and the runners, the ducks and the trees, and—as their backdrop—the New York City buildings.

"Hey, you two, get together and look here," Sarah said. "Let me take your picture!"

Fallon and Pluto stood together on top of their rock, overlooking the park, the city, everything, and Fallon pulled Pluto close. They both said, "Cheese!" and Sarah took the picture, and Fallon helped Pluto climb back down.

"I'll text this to your dad so he can see it and send it to your mom," Sarah said. "She'll love this."

Pluto froze, as Fallon ran over to Sarah to ask if she could see the photo, too.

She hadn't thought about her mom once all day.

Pluto's dad met them back at his apartment an hour after they got back from their day out in the city. He brought boxes of pizza he said were "the best pizza in the city, so the best pizza in the world," which made Pluto frown, even though she ate it without comment.

"Can you teach us how to play D&D after dinner?" Fallon had a long string of cheese dangling from her mouth to the pizza in her hand, and she talked even as she tried to eat it.

Pluto's dad pointed an excited finger in Fallon's direction, as he said to Pluto, "I like this kid! She's a good find, Pluto Jean!"

Fallon swallowed the cheese, ducking her head to try and hide her smile.

There are about two hundred *billion* galaxies in the known universe, and our galaxy is home to at least one hundred billion planets. Still, Pluto ended up on this planet, this Earth. And out of the 1.3 million identified species on Earth, Pluto and Fallon both ended up as people on the same New Jersey boardwalk. When all of Pluto's friendships were falling apart, when she didn't know how to be a good friend, Fallon had walked through the pizzeria door.

Fallon wasn't just a good find, Pluto thought. She was an astronomical one.

"John, put something more fun on the speakers for the girls," Sarah said, as another instrumental piece began to play.

Her dad's expression was dramatically comical, his mouth dropping and his eyes opening wide. "Excuse me! This is a great song!" He turned the volume up, sounds of piano bouncing around the room. "The composer is a local Jersey guy. Your mom swears she's served him pizza, but I think she's full of it."

"If he's local, he's had our pizza," Pluto said. "Everyone eats our pizza."

"You can't dance to this," Sarah complained. "What fun is pizza if we can't have a dance party to go with it?"

Her dad scoffed, holding out a hand for Pluto. "Let's show her we can dance to this, Pluto Jean. Come here."

She hesitated, but then took his hand. He pulled her up off the couch and put one of her hands on his shoulder, then held the other tight. His other hand went to her waist and they began swaying. "See? We're dancing," he said.

Sarah laughed. "Yeah, well, I guess you are." She turned to Fallon. "May I have this dance?"

Fallon blushed and nodded.

The four of them slow danced around the living room, around the coffee table, doing their best not to bump into the TV. Pluto's dad spun her. "There you go, Pluto Jean," he said. "Let the emotions of the song fill you all the way up and move to it."

Pluto's eyebrows knit together. "What emotions? It's just music. There's no words."

"Listen to the music," he said. "It's all there. There's a lot of love in this song. He wrote it for his husband, and you don't need words for that. Think about how it makes you feel."

Pluto didn't like thinking about how things made her feel.

Still, she listened to the music, to the feel of her dad's arms, so much bigger and different than her mom's, even so much different than she remembered. She couldn't recall the last time he'd held her, but she also couldn't remember the last time she was held tight by her mom without one of them needing consoling, without it being something heavier and not nearly as simple as a dance.

Pluto started wondering what the limitations would be of music in space. She would have to call the Hayden Planetarium Astronomy Question and Answer Hotline and ask. Could this musician from Jersey play his piano in zero gravity? Would the song sound the same? Or would it be muted and dim like a weak constellation?

"Let me cut in," Sarah suddenly said, and Pluto's dad spun her to Fallon as he took Sarah into his arms.

Pluto watched them dance, simple and fun, Sarah's soft laugh filling the room alongside the music.

Fallon put her hand on Pluto's waist, and Pluto jumped. "Sorry!" Fallon said. "I just . . . can we dance?"

Pluto nodded and took Fallon's hand. Fallon wasn't much taller than Pluto, and it was easier, it felt less awkward and more right, to place her hand on Fallon's shoulder than her dad's.

The flutters in Pluto's stomach felt nice.

They danced around the living room, and when the

song came to an end, they kept going as the next song began. They danced, and danced, and danced, the car horns and life of the city drowned out by the music and their laughter.

That night, Pluto did not miss the stars. She didn't even remember they weren't visible.

Her mom came the next morning before lunchtime. Pluto had already taken a shower and her medication. She was sitting on the floor with Fallon and her dad around the coffee table, absorbed in a beginner's D&D campaign they had started (slowly, since there was a lot to do and learn and create and understand first) last night.

"Didn't expect you so early," Pluto's dad said as he answered the door. "We're in the middle of a campaign."

"I told you I didn't want to get stuck in traffic," her mom said, and looked past him toward Pluto. "And, self-ishly, I really missed my Shooting Star."

Pluto's disappointment shocked her. The feeling in her chest that squeezed at the thought of leaving felt . . . wrong. But it was there, and it was real, and Pluto—who hadn't wanted to come in the first place—didn't want to leave now that it was time.

Sarah took out her hand sanitizer and rubbed her

hands. "Hi," she said, standing and extending a bacteria-free hand toward Pluto's mom. "I'm Sarah."

Her mom hesitated for a brief moment. "Oh! Hi," she said, shaking Sarah's hand. "I'm Anna, Pluto's mom. It's great to finally meet you."

"You want to stay for lunch before you go?" Sarah asked.

"Oh, thanks, that's sweet, but we really should go." Her mom gestured at Pluto. "Plu, you and Fallon get your stuff packed so I can talk to your dad for a minute."

Pluto's dad rolled his eyes dramatically. "As you can see, she's in one piece, Anna. She was fine. She did good. We did great, actually, no issues or anything at all."

Were they really going to do this now? Here? In front of Fallon and Sarah?

"I see that, but—"

"Just, think about what I said, okay?" her dad interrupted. "Sarah's got pictures of the kid out in the middle of Central Park. She *likes* it here. It's good for her here."

Her mom's shoulders were squared for battle. "Can you just help me get all their stuff? I'm double parked again."

"Fine, Anna," Pluto's dad said, crossing the room to his office. Pluto's mom told her to "just . . . stay here" as she followed Pluto's dad. She closed the office door behind her, and Pluto knew they were going to argue, knew that the good feelings she'd had all day yesterday, all morning, were going to go away.

Fallon rolled the dice around in her hands, and Sarah pretended she wasn't listening, and Pluto stood in the center of her dad's apartment, waiting for her parents to stop fighting, wishing she could just go back to bed.

That night, back home, Pluto counted the thirty-two chips in the gray paint on her wall, over and over and over. Thirty-two paint chips. Thirty-two stars pulled down. Pluto hated those paint chips. She hated her walls. She wondered if her dad would let her paint the ones in his office if they decided she would go stay with him.

Pluto turned to face the threshold of her bedroom, where her door used to be before her mom knocked it down, knocking Pluto's world upside down with it. Her mom was in her own room, and Pluto's list was in her hamper in the pocket of her jeans.

If she went outside, right now, she'd be able to see the city across the bay from the boardwalk. If she looked out her window, right here, she'd see stars.

Her mom hugged her tighter than usual when they got home from her dad's, and it made Pluto feel guilty. The entire car ride home she was thinking about how, after fighting it all summer, living in the city with her dad might not actually be all that bad.

Mrs. McAuliffe was going over social studies with Pluto, which made Pluto smile, because Christa McAuliffe had taught social studies, and her Mrs. McAuliffe was really good at teaching it, too. She started singing a song called "King Tut" and Pluto laughed, and Mrs. McAuliffe looked at her like she was the best student in the world. Pluto liked that, too.

"You seem extra happy today," Mrs. McAuliffe noted.

"I had a really good weekend at my dad's," Pluto said.

"Hmm," said Mrs. McAuliffe. "That's interesting. You didn't seem too happy about having to go last week."

"It *was* unexpected," Pluto agreed. "But Fallon came,

171

and my dad's girlfriend has OCD, and the city was really busy and noisy, and I was busy and noisy there, too, and I felt like me. Like the old me."

Mrs. McAuliffe smiled. "I'm really glad to hear that. Sometimes it takes time for medications to work, and sometimes you just need to wait for that light at the end of a long, long, sad tunnel."

The word made Pluto think of the Lincoln Tunnel, and made her think of the city. She smiled even bigger. "I thought I would feel worse in the city, but I didn't. I felt better."

Mrs. McAuliffe frowned a bit, which made Pluto frown a bit, because what had she said that made the smile go away?

Little bumps on the front door, followed by the sound of the doorknob opening, signaled Sunny's arrival home. She stumbled in with her arms full of grocery bags. "Oh! Hello, Pluto!" Her voice was muffled behind all the bags.

"Wait, Sunny, jeez. Let me help you." Mrs. McAuliffe was up off the couch quickly, and she hurried over to take some bags from Sunny, who laughed when her face was finally free. Mrs. McAuliffe laughed, too, and they seemed to share a little private moment, even though Pluto laughed a little with them. They reminded Pluto of her and Fallon, and she liked that. She hoped she could have such a good friend when she was their age. She really hoped it would still be Fallon—or maybe even she and Meredith could be friends again someday.

And then Pluto watched as they kissed.

Right on the lips.

Oh.

"What was that, Plu?" Mrs. McAuliffe asked.

Pluto didn't realize she said anything out loud, but she *did* realize she was still staring. "Nothing!" she said, but her voice was high, a little too high. The real Christa McAuliffe, from the *Challenger*, had a husband and two kids.

This Mrs. McAuliffe didn't have a husband. Which meant . . . she had a wife.

And this Mrs. McAuliffe and Sunny still reminded Pluto of her and Fallon.

"Plu, come on, we gotta get a move on."

It was early, and Pluto wanted to keep sleeping, wanted to be left alone.

"Did you take your meds? Come on, Plu, seriously, we have to open up shop," her mom said from where she stood in Pluto's doorway, putting on her earrings. "Donna can't be there this morning, I already told you this. We gotta go."

Get a move on. Come on, Plu. We gotta go. Move, move, move.

Pluto sank into her bed just as her mom flipped her bedroom light on. Pluto pulled at her comforter, trying to block out the sudden brightness.

"I'm not messing around. We need to go."

We need to go. Get a move on. Get. A. Move. On.

"Pluto!"

"Leave me alone!" Pluto screamed at the top of her lungs. "Go away and *leave me alone!*"

Her mom stared at her from the doorway, jaw dropped, until she pulled herself together. "Don't yell at me. You have to get out of bed."

Pluto sat up, reached for her pillow, and threw it at the doorway, at the space where there would normally be a door (a door she would slam if she had one), at the space where her mom was still standing. Her mom ducked out of the way, shocked. "I don't want to get out of bed!" Pluto yelled. "I'm not getting out of bed! What was the point of hiring Donna if you still need to make me do things I don't want to do!"

"Hey!" her mom yelled back, crossing to Pluto's bed. "Knock it off." She reached for Pluto's arm, but Pluto started kicking her. "Pluto, stop!"

"Get off me!" Pluto yelled, kicking, as tears spilled

down her cheeks and her chest grew tight and her head started pounding. "I want to be left alone! *Dad* would leave me alone!"

"Yeah, no kidding! Your dad's left you alone for thirteen years!"

It was a low blow, and her mom cringed as the words left her mouth. She knew it was a low blow, too. Pluto pushed at her. "He doesn't make things worse. *You* make things worse."

"I'm trying to help."

"You suck at it!" Pluto backed away from her mom, pressing herself against the wall where the stars used to be. "I lied to you on my birthday, I *hated* the planetarium, I hated every second of it and I hate being dragged to the pizzeria, and I hate every second of being here right now with you!"

Her mom took a step away from the bed, her hands raised weakly, as if in surrender. Tears streamed down her face, her eyes wide, gray irises like storm clouds. "I don't know what to do," her mom said, voice cracking. "I'm *trying* . . . I can't . . . I don't know what to do."

Pluto pulled her knees into her chest, trying to take deep breaths and failing. "I want to live with Dad," she said.

Her mom looked as though she was the one

having trouble breathing. "You . . . what?" she practically whispered.

Pluto couldn't say it a second time.

"But . . . your list," her mom said, cheeks wet, shaking her head.

Pluto had failed at almost everything on her list. She was tired of trying. She was tired of her mom's desperate, eager eyes. She was tired of all of it. "Get out of my room," she yelled. "I want you out of my room. I want a door again so you *stay out of my room!*"

"Okay!" her mom yelled, and then took a deep breath to control her voice. "Okay," she said much softer.

Her mom didn't immediately go. She stood there, in the empty doorway, tearstained and pale, and when she did turn to leave, when Pluto was finally alone, Pluto did not feel any better.

She buried herself in her comforter, closing her eyes and finding the darkness, shutting everything out to go back to sleep.

Pluto still didn't want to get out of bed the next morning, but not because her body protested. She was mad, it was pushing at her chest, and she didn't know how to face her mom. When she finally did leave her room, there was a bowl waiting for her at her seat at the table, the cereal box beside it. Pluto could hear that her mom was already in the bathroom they shared, getting ready for the day.

Pluto didn't want to go into the bathroom; she didn't want to look into the mirror at her mom's reflection, too afraid of what she might see in her eyes. So she took a seat, poured herself some cereal, and focused on the newspaper left on the table.

It was open to an article about the Perseid meteor shower. Which made Pluto mad, because her mom clearly did that on purpose, clearly tried to extend an olive branch that wasn't really an olive branch, that felt more like another ambush.

The Perseid meteor shower could be seen from the beaches in Monmouth County every year in August. It was tradition, just like going to the planetarium on Pluto's birthday, for her and her mom to watch the shooting stars together. Her mom must have wanted to keep tradition, must have wanted Pluto to want to try.

Pluto felt her chest grow tight, her jaw clench, and she threw the newspaper across the room, pages scattering to the floor. She didn't want to try. She was tired of trying, even more tired of failing. She'd failed at the planetarium, she'd failed at the therapist, she'd failed at being Meredith's friend.

She'd failed at everything here.

She suddenly felt like she was being watched, and she turned around to find her mom standing in the threshold to the kitchen, staring at her with wide, teary eyes. But then her mom blinked, and the tears went away, and her jaw was set as she said, "Go get changed. We're leaving in fifteen minutes."

It was a long ride to the restaurant, even though it was right around the corner, and by the time they got there, Pluto couldn't handle it anymore. She didn't want to be near her mom, to feel her eyes on her, to wonder what on earth she could be thinking. "I don't want to be at the stupid restaurant."

"Tough," her mom said.

"I said I don't want to—"

"I heard you, Pluto," her mom snapped.

Pluto yanked her seat belt off and shoved open the door. "Then I'm going to go see Fallon."

"Fine," her mom called after her. "And work on that attitude while you're gone."

The summer was half over, but Pluto realized as she headed toward Fallon's that she hadn't gone down the boardwalk toward the amusement park at all this year. Usually—like last year—Pluto would have ridden the roller coasters and the go-karts and begged her mom for dollars so that she and Meredith could try to win prizes from the games a million times by now. It was where she and Meredith challenged each other at Skee-Ball last year. Where they spent the entire summer they turned ten saving up tickets (and stealing all the unclaimed tickets from the game machines) for the popcorn machine that *everyone* wanted to save enough tickets for. Where Jeremy Ng kissed Meredith, and after, where she and Pluto hid behind the claw machines to gossip about what his mouth felt like.

Thinking about all that just made Pluto feel even angrier, and she bit hard into the side of her cheek.

"Pluto!"

She turned at the sound of Fallon's voice, and Fallon's smile pulled Pluto's mind from memories of the past *her* to something much better.

"What're you doing here?" Fallon asked. She had powdered sugar on her hands and cheek.

Pluto stepped forward to wipe the powder off Fallon's face. Fallon's cheeks turned pink under Pluto's fingers. "Can I hang in your store today?"

"I was hoping to spend my break at yours," Fallon said. "My brothers are driving me up a wall."

Pluto sighed. "I don't want to be anywhere near my mom."

Fallon's eyebrows shot up. "Really? Why?"

"We're fighting. I don't want to talk about it, okay?" It came out harsher than she meant it, but Pluto couldn't bring herself to apologize. Her chest still felt too tight.

Fallon slowly nodded. "Okay. I guess you can come help me make zeppoles?"

Fallon's dad did not want Pluto anywhere near the hot oil, which was a fair rule, since Pluto did not want to be anywhere near it, either. So she, along with Fallon's little brother Tommy, were in charge of the powdered sugar while Fallon was in charge of the zeppole dough.

Fallon's family, the Zamprognas, worked much differently than Pluto and her mom. For one, it was just them, no college students helping out, no other cooks or employees, no Donna. For two, there were more of them. Fallon had a mom and a dad who mostly liked each other, and two older brothers and two younger ones. Her oldest brother, Grant, was too busy planning his new life with his fiancée to work with them, and Fallon's other older brother, Dom, constantly got in trouble for disappearing up the boardwalk with his friends. Tommy and Billy, though, who were eight and ten, spent their summer in the store like Pluto and Fallon did.

Billy was currently sitting at a table outside, working on the summer schoolwork he had to finish if he wanted to pass math and get into fifth grade. He looked sullen and bitter about it. Pluto could relate.

The Zamprognas were loud, and big, and Pluto

wondered what it might be like to grow up in a family that wasn't just her and her mom.

"Here, Pluto, eat one of these. I think they're gross, but apparently everyone else loves fried Twinkies," Mrs. Zamprogna said, handing Pluto a plastic plate with a gooey fried Twinkie, covered with too much powdered sugar, thanks to Tommy. Pluto didn't really want it, but she didn't want to say no to Mrs. Zamprogna, either. She was tall and round, with an apron stretched around her middle and her hair pulled back from her face. She had a soft look that reminded Pluto of a *mom*—not a particular mom, just a mom in general.

"Can I take a break while Pluto eats it?" Fallon asked, wiping the sweat off her forehead with her forearm.

Her mom gave them the go-ahead, and they went outside to sit on the wooden benches. They waved at Billy, who was daydreaming out at the ocean instead of focusing on his homework. Pluto picked at her Twinkie.

"Have you talked to your dad since the weekend?" Fallon asked. "We should go back sometime. I want to play D&D again. I want to learn to be the game master, so I can come up with the stories. Speaking of! I was on the computer, there's a *ton* of awesome bookstores maybe we could check out next time. There's one that has *eighteen miles* of books!"

Pluto shook her head. "I don't want to talk about my dad's right now."

"Okay," Fallon said. "Well, what about your list? Is there anything you wanna try and cross off? Isn't your friend's party soon? Oh! Maybe we can go to the gift shops and find her a present?"

Pluto scowled. She suddenly felt really, really angry again, her shoulders and chest tight. "I don't want to talk about that either."

Fallon's eyebrows pinched together, confused. "Oh. Okay. Well, can we talk about my list? I was hoping you could help me figure out how to talk to my mom about the dress thing."

"I don't want to talk about the stupid lists at *all*, Fallon," Pluto snapped. "I don't even know if I want to do them anymore. And I don't want this Twinkie, either." She pushed the paper plate away from her, powdered sugar getting all over the table.

"What are you—" Fallon shook her head. "What's wrong? I thought we were spending the summer on these lists. I thought this was the point of everything."

"Maybe the point was to just be friends," Pluto said, her nose burning as she held back tears.

"It was—it *is*—I just . . ." Fallon looked as though she might start crying, too, and Pluto couldn't help thinking of the fight with her mom. "What's going on? I don't understand what's wrong."

"*I'm* wrong!" Pluto shouted. "And everything was okay in the city, so why should I keep failing at that stupid list when I can just forget all of it and go stay with my dad?"

Fallon narrowed her eyes, shoulders tensing. "You want to stay with your . . . After everything we've . . ." She couldn't seem to finish any of her sentences. "Is this why you're fighting with your mom? Your dad was hardly even *there* last weekend!"

"You don't understand!" Pluto was shouting, but she couldn't bring herself to care if anyone could overhear her, if even the seagulls were startled enough to turn and stare. "All you had to do was get a stupid haircut. You have no *idea* what it's like!"

"You know what, Pluto," Fallon said, standing. "You're right. I don't understand. But neither do you. So, forget it. You don't want to do the list, *fine*. I don't want your help anyway."

Fallon left so quickly Pluto couldn't stop her. She couldn't say, *I'm sorry* and *I didn't mean to upset you* and *I don't know what I'm doing anymore.*

She didn't know how to say, *I've hurt my best friend and I've hurt my mom and I didn't mean to hurt you, too.*

Instead, she watched Fallon walk away, caught between wanting to apologize and wanting to keep on yelling.

Pluto could not stay near the funnel cake shop. She did not want to go back to the pizzeria, either.

So there she stood, against an ice cream shop in the center of the boardwalk, on a busy summer day, jaw and fists and eyes clenched tight, breathing heavily through the tightness in her chest, wishing she could just be invisible so that no one would stop and ask her if she was okay, because she didn't think she was okay, but if she opened her mouth to answer them, she might just start screaming.

She wished the Hayden Planetarium Astronomy Question and Answer Hotline had answered her question months ago and told her how to create a black hole so she could fall into it.

She wanted to be left alone, but she didn't want to *feel* lonely. She couldn't get herself to just . . . be *normal*. To just be Pluto. To just be the girl she used to be, before this summer, before the diagnosis, who was fun and kind and friendly. Who loved to listen to her mom talk about outer space. Who loved running down the boardwalk with Meredith.

"Pluto? Are you okay?"

A soft hand touched Pluto's shoulder, and Pluto jumped, her eyes flying open to see Meredith jump, too.

Pluto was having trouble breathing. Meredith grabbed her hand, but Pluto yanked it away. She couldn't help it. She didn't want Meredith, or anyone, touching her. She was just so . . . *mad*. At her mom. At Fallon. At Meredith. At *everyone*.

"Do you need me to get your mom?"

"No," Pluto managed to choke out. "Just . . . *no*."

Meredith didn't say anything else, but she didn't leave, either. They stood silently against the wall of the ice cream shop. It was cloudy, a slow day for the boardwalk, and Pluto counted the people who walked by, trying to control her breathing. Two boys on their skateboards skated in between an older couple walking hand in hand, forcing them to release their hold. Near them, a little kid was throwing a hissy fit over her dropped ice cream, and a dog was trying desperately, straining at its leash, to lick it up.

Mercury, Venus, Earth, and Mars . . .

"Remember the time Harper's dog got lost, and we searched for hours on the boardwalk trying to find her?" Meredith suddenly said.

Pluto nodded. She did remember. Harper cried the whole time, and Pluto and Meredith decided to ride the rocket roller coaster, the highest point on the boardwalk, to try to spot her. Pluto, from the very top of that coaster, saw the dog first. "She was on the beach," Pluto said. "Chasing seagulls."

"Such a dumb dog," Meredith said. "Remember how, after that, we called the planetarium hotline and asked them how to successfully launch a dog into space?"

"Harper was *so* mad," Pluto said.

"Are you okay?" Meredith asked.

"Yeah," Pluto nodded. "Thanks."

Meredith chewed the inside of her cheek. "What's wrong with you, Pluto? Just . . . tell me."

"You already know. I have depression. And anxiety."

Meredith sighed. "I know. But what's *wrong*? Why does that stop you from being my friend? Why are you friends with the funnel cake girl and not me?"

Pluto looked up at Meredith, whose light brown eyes were wide and pleading. Fallon's eyes were the color of Neptune, and Pluto's were the color of Mercury, but Meredith's were the color of Pluto. And that . . . that meant something. All those years of friendship meant something.

"Fallon didn't know me before," she admitted. "She couldn't tell that I'm different now."

Meredith grew quiet, looking out at the ocean. At the city skyline that felt, right then, even farther away. "I just miss my friend." Meredith turned to look back at Pluto.

"I'm sorry I got mad at you. It just hurt. I was . . . jealous, I guess. And confused."

"I'm sorry, too," Pluto said. "For making you feel that way."

"I should go, though." Meredith cringed. "I told my mom I was going to the bathroom, like, forever ago. She's gonna start worrying."

"Oh," Pluto said. "Yeah, okay."

"But—" Meredith took a deep breath. "You should come to my birthday party. If you can, I mean. If you want to." She smiled, even if it was a little wobbly. "I really do want you there."

Take medication. Visit the planetarium with Mom.

Go to Meredith's birthday party.

Meredith was giving her the chance to actually accomplish something on her list. If that was something she wanted to do.

Pluto took a deep breath. She didn't feel quite so mad anymore.

"Okay," she said. "Yeah. I'll try."

"You're not even trying today, Pluto. Why're you looking so sad?" Mrs. McAuliffe asked about a half hour into their tutoring session.

Pluto scowled. "I have depression. I *always* look sad." Or angry, or tired, or anything other than what a normal thirteen-year-old girl in the summertime should look like.

But Mrs. McAuliffe shook her head. "You know what I mean. This is different. What's bothering you? Because I know something is bothering you. That last math question had an entire space station theme and you didn't even crack a smile."

Did it? Pluto read back over the last couple of questions.

One was about the square footage of materials a guy needed to build a porch, and the other was about the amount of flour someone needed to bake a cake. "There's no space station question."

"Aha! But you had to read them again. Which proves to me you're not even a little bit paying attention," Mrs. McAuliffe said. She looked proud of herself. "What's going on?"

Pluto sighed. "Everyone is mad at me. Well, I made everyone mad at me. Well, I yelled at my mom and at my friend Fallon and now they're both mad at me."

"Why did you yell at them?"

"I don't know," Pluto said.

"You're going to need to do better than that if you're going to ignore my math lessons all day," Mrs. McAuliffe responded.

Pluto ran her fingers over the pages in her math workbook, along the edges, before turning the page back to the beginning. "I don't know," she said again, honestly. "I was just so mad that things were so good when I was with my dad and then I came back home and it went back to normal. Or not *normal*, but back to being bad again." Pluto sighed. "Which I guess *is* normal. And then I couldn't make the mad feelings go away."

Mrs. McAuliffe *hmm*ed in that way she did when she was taking in everything Pluto was saying. She always *hmm*ed when Pluto spoke to her. It made Pluto feel like she was a very good listener. Not everyone was. "Have you tried talking to your mom or Fallon? Explain to them how you felt in the moment and why, and that you are sorry if you hurt their feelings? They know you, Plu. They know you didn't mean it."

"I never *mean* to do anything lately," Pluto said, her chest tightening with that familiar anger all over again.

"You're seeing a therapist, right?"

Pluto pulled a face.

Mrs. McAuliffe laughed. "No! No. Therapy can be great! Scary and uncomfortable, at least at first, but really great. Your therapist is *yours*. To say anything to. All of this, and more. You might find you really like it."

Pluto shook her head. "I tried. It didn't go so well."

"You should try again," Mrs. McAuliffe said. "When you're ready."

Pluto leaned back into the soft cushions of Mrs. McAuliffe's couch, pouting a little, sulking a little more than that. She glanced around the living room, at the photographs along the mantel above the small fireplace. They were all of Mrs. McAuliffe and Sunny, laughing at the beach, or at a restaurant, or in the city with the big Christmas tree in the background.

Looking at them made Pluto's chest feel tight again. Because they made her think of Fallon on the boardwalk, or Fallon at the pizzeria, or Fallon by her side in the city.

"Mrs. McAuliffe?" Pluto said, her voice suddenly much quieter. "How did you know you really really liked someone like Sunny?"

Mrs. McAuliffe smirked. "You mean how did I know I really liked someone beautiful and funny and smart and, well, a bit kooky?"

Pluto sighed. No, that's not what she meant. But also it was. But also it wasn't.

Mrs. McAuliffe knew what she was asking anyway. "I just did, Pluto. It just felt right. A lot of things in my life didn't, but Sunny? She always did."

Pluto didn't know what to say to that, but she nodded anyway, and reached to pull her math notebook closer to her. She picked up her pencil. "Yeah," she said. "I think I get that."

She didn't say anything more about fighting with her mom and Fallon, or Sunny, or how some of those things were connected. And Mrs. McAuliffe didn't ask her to.

Later that night, even though every inch of her was fighting it, Pluto took a deep breath and knocked softly on her mom's bedroom door. "Mom?"

Her mom put down the book she was reading. Tried, and failed, to hide the eagerness on her face.

It made Pluto's stomach hurt. "I was wondering. I mean, I know I keep messing up, but I think I'd like to try again. I mean . . ." The words were getting jumbled in her head.

"Tell me, Shooting Star," her mom said. "Whatever it is."

Pluto thought about everything Mrs. McAuliffe had told her, and she tried again. "Can we make another therapy appointment?"

This seemed to shock her mom, who put her book down on the dresser beside her, full attention on Pluto. "Really? I mean . . . That's what you want?"

"Well . . . it's on my list," she said.

The look on her mom's face made Pluto feel like she might start crying. "It is on your list," Pluto's mom agreed. "I thought—I mean, are you . . . still working on your list?"

Pluto slowly nodded.

"So . . ." Her mom was being careful with her words. Pluto wished she wouldn't. She wished she would talk to

Pluto like normal, without walking on eggshells. "What does that mean . . . about your dad's?"

It was the question Pluto was waiting for, but the one she still didn't have an answer to. Did she really want to leave her mom? Her home? The boardwalk? Fallon?

But things had seemed so . . . easy, in New York.

"I don't know," Pluto answered honestly. "I just . . . want to do the list."

"Okay," her mom said, a little too quickly. "Then we'll do the list. And I'll make that appointment first thing in the morning."

Now was the time Pluto would normally climb into her mom's bed, into her mom's arms, and let her mom tell her about the universe. About Pluto's place in it.

Instead, she hovered by the door. "I'm gonna go to bed," she said.

Her mom nodded. "Goodnight, Plu."

"Goodnight, Mom."

Take medication. Get into the 8th grade. Watch the Perseid meteor shower with Mom. See the therapist. Go to Meredith's birthday party.

New list. New day. Pluto was ready to start again.

That didn't mean she was ready for her mom to wake

up and schedule a therapy appointment for that morning, but there she was, once again in the waiting room, gripping the arms of an uncomfortable chair.

New list. New day. Second chance.

"You look like you're getting ready for battle," her mom said with a slight frown. "You're safe here. She's not going to breathe fire at you or anything, I swear, Plu. Even if she did, you know she'd have to answer to me."

Pluto wasn't afraid of the therapist. She was afraid that her second attempt would go as miserably as the first. The thought of failure made her want to give up before it could happen, made her want to turn around and walk out the door.

"Pluto Timoney?" the receptionist called.

New list. New day. Second chance.

She took a deep breath. She didn't know if she was ready. But even the best astronauts got nervous before takeoff.

If they could travel outside the safe haven of Earth and into the unknown . . . so could she.

"Hello again, Pluto," Dr. Collins said, her wide mouth in a kind smile as she pulled her glasses off her face. She motioned, once again, to the bright red couch across from her. "You want to sit down this time? Might be more comfortable."

Pluto eyed the couch, then the door, then Dr. Collins.

Dr. Collins laughed gently. "You can keep standing if you want. Makes it easier for a quick getaway, I completely understand." She stood, crossing from behind her desk to perch on the front of it. She crossed her heels, bringing Pluto's attention to the work boots that did not match the rest of her outfit—professional blouse and dress pants—at all. They did, however, match her messy hair.

Dr. Collins followed Pluto's gaze. "I usually change these when I get here, even though my heels kill my feet, but I've been swamped today and I keep forgetting."

"I like them," Pluto said.

"Your mom said it was your idea for this appointment today," Dr. Collins said. "And that you wanted to see me alone. There must be something you want to talk to me about."

Pluto tilted her head. "I thought you're supposed to ask me a bunch of questions."

Dr. Collins laughed. "I can do that, too. But I have a feeling there's something you want to get off your chest, and I don't want to waste your time. So, you can take the lead if you want. Or I can take it for you. What do you think, Pluto?"

"Did you know that a girl my age picked the name Pluto? For the planet, I mean," Pluto suddenly found herself saying. She didn't even know why she was bringing it up.

Dr. Collins looked impressed. "I didn't know that. That's really cool."

"My mom named me," Pluto said. "I was born six weeks early, and I was the smallest baby in the nursery at the hospital. There were eight other babies. I was the ninth. I was Pluto."

"I like that," Dr. Collins said. She did not comment on the fact that Pluto was not really a planet, not anymore. "I was named after my great-grandmother. Which isn't as fun. She was really nasty, from what I understand, but my mom thought she was hilarious and hoped that I would grow up to be just as fierce, I guess."

Pluto smiled. She liked that, too. "The Hayden Planetarium, the one in the city that's in the Department of Astrophysics, it has some of the smartest people in the world working there. They have a hotline, and sometimes we, I mean, Meredith and me, we called to ask questions, but lately they haven't been able to . . ." Pluto paused, her smile dropping, her hand rubbing the fabric of the sofa next to her. "Dr. Collins?"

"Yes, Pluto?"

"Mrs. McAuliffe . . . my tutor Mrs. McAuliffe, not the one who . . . Anyway, she said that you could help me. So, could you, please? Could you please help fix me?"

Dr. Collins exhaled, her smile and eyes soft and . . . kind of sad. "What does that mean to you? To be 'fixed'?"

"I don't want to have a diagnosis anymore."

"Pluto . . ."

"Please, can't you help me? I just want to be better. That's why I came back. That's why I'm here." Pluto reached into her back pocket, pulling out her list, still wrinkled and worn and ripped, with some things scratched out and new things added. "I made this list. Everything I'm supposed to do by the end of the summer to be me again. I need help with this. Please, I need you to help me do this."

Dr. Collins reached out a hand. "Let's see what you've got."

Pluto handed her the list, and her stomach did flips while Dr. Collins read it all, read all of the things that Pluto needed to do.

"Are you taking your medication?" Dr. Collins asked.

Pluto nodded emphatically. "Yes. Well, sometimes I just sleep. But I always try to take them."

"And here you are, visiting me."

"Well, I messed up the first time."

Dr. Collins looked at Pluto with that kind smile again.

"Hey, there's nothing wrong with a bad session. It happens, Pluto. To adults, too. It's hard to be here, and you coming back was very brave." She focused on the list. "This one is crossed out?"

"My birthday already happened. The planetarium didn't go so well. I usually love it, but I *hated* it this time. It made me feel all anxious." Pluto sighed. "But there's this meteor shower coming up. The Perseids. It orbits around and comes back every year. We can see it best in the middle of August. My mom and I, well, she loves it. And we watch it together every year, just like we go to the planetarium every year. I don't want to hate this, too. I don't want to keep ruining the things my mom loves, too."

"Hmm," said Dr. Collins. It reminded Pluto of Mrs. McAuliffe, and suddenly, it felt a little easier to breathe. "Do you like space, Pluto?"

"Yeah, a lot. A *lot*, a lot. Ever since I was little my mom would read me books about astronomy and space, and we would watch documentaries on YouTube and Netflix. We used to close the pizzeria at night and wander close to the beach and look for shooting stars when the sky was clear enough." Pluto paused. "Not anymore, though. We haven't really done any of that lately."

"Why do you think that is?" Dr. Collins asked.

Pluto frowned. "I don't know. Everything's been hard. Ever since the doctor diagnosed me."

Dr. Collins tilted her head to the side. "Only since then?"

"What?"

Dr. Collins flipped through the files on her desk. "You were diagnosed a few months ago. Were things easier before then?"

Pluto thought about it. "No," she admitted. "It wasn't a good school year."

"Your mom said you had a hard time keeping your grades up."

She did. She'd had a hard time doing her homework before tutoring even came into the picture. And things with Meredith were hard long before Pluto started medication. "Before that, then. Things were easier before that."

"Did your depression and anxiety start just this past school year, then?"

Pluto frowned deeper. She slowly sank into the red sofa. "No. I mean . . . no. I used to get angry all the time, for no reason. Or really sad. Or . . . I've always slept a lot. Poppy used to say that I was just like my grandma."

"When did he say this?"

"He died when I was five. My mom told me I remind her of my grandma a lot, too, though."

Dr. Collins had a small smile on her face, and she leaned closer to Pluto, as if confiding a secret. "Sometimes the chemicals in your brain change as you grow. Especially when your hormones start fluctuating, and you're just about at that age. As you get older, things like harder schoolwork and busier schedules can be factors in your mental health. And different people have different factors that can, and sometimes do, play a part, like the stress you feel when navigating between your mom and your dad. It doesn't mean you were a different person before the diagnosis. It just means we now have an explanation for all the things you were feeling, and continue to feel."

Pluto scratched at the soft fabric of the sofa. "Do you think . . . Was my grandma depressed, too, then?"

"That's very possible. Sometimes these things run in families. But it's something you're going to have to talk to your mom about, and I encourage you to do that," Dr. Collins said. "And, Pluto, I want you to listen to me very carefully, okay? Having depression, feeling anxious and sad and angry because of it, is not something you need to be ashamed of." Pluto looked down at her feet, but Dr. Collins was not having any of that. "Hey, listen. You have *nothing* to be ashamed of. Upwards of thirteen percent of twelve- to seventeen-year-olds have suffered from some kind of major depression. You're not alone, and there is nothing wrong with having to be here talking to me, or having to take your medication, or having to figure out how to bridge the gap between the Pluto you thought you knew before your diagnosis and the Pluto you are now."

"I don't want to bridge the gap," Pluto said. "I just want to be Pluto."

"You *still are* Pluto," Dr. Collins said. "You just need to learn how to care for and accept this new understanding of you."

CRITERION #3

A PLANET MUST CLEAR ITS ORBIT OF SMALLER OBJECTS SO THAT THERE IS NOTHING IN ITS PATH.

20

Pluto's mom was arguing with Mrs. McAuliffe. Which felt . . . wrong. Absolutely wrong and totally weird and Pluto didn't know if she wanted to go make sure her mom was okay or to go make her mom leave Mrs. McAuliffe alone.

They'd sent her into Mrs. McAuliffe's kitchen, where Sunny was getting her a glass of water and some cookies, because Mrs. McAuliffe's kitchen had a door that separated it from the living room. Pluto could hear them anyway, though. Could hear the way her mom's voice rose in pitch and could hear, very clearly, the things they were saying. "I just thought it would be important that you know. I want her to feel safe with me, and comfortable sharing things with me, but I worry. Suicide rates are so much higher for kids who are queer and—"

"Do *not* say that word," Pluto's mom interrupted.

"Queer?"

"*Suicide*," her mom corrected, her voice tense and tight. "She's *thirteen*. Thirteen! And I will not . . . She will not . . . This is why we're going through everything we are now! To take care of her. To *protect* her. You're her *tutor*, and you're overstepping."

Pluto leaned closer to the door.

"Hey." Sunny's hand was suddenly on Pluto's shoulder, and Pluto jumped. "Sorry. But come on, come pick out a cookie. We've got, like, every kind of Oreo known to man."

Pluto looked back at the closed door.

Sunny sighed, following her gaze. "I don't know why they think the door is soundproof. Your mom's just scared, Pluto. She loves you very much. And Lucy cares, too, and that's why—"

"Lucy?" Pluto interrupted, startled. It hadn't occurred to her that Mrs. McAuliffe had a first name—one that was *hers* and not Christa's.

Pluto's mom burst into the kitchen. Her face was flushed, her gray eyes cloudy. "Come on, Plu. We gotta get going."

Pluto had a million things to say to her mom, and she knew her mom must have had a million things to say to her, but apparently they were not going to say any of those things to each other. Pluto's mom asked Pluto what she wanted for dinner, and Pluto shrugged, and her mom started talking about romaine lettuce for about a half hour before Pluto excused herself to her room.

After dinner, Pluto was listening to a podcast when her mom called to her. "Plu? Your dad's on the phone."

Pluto padded into the living room, where her mom was sitting on the sofa. She took the phone, ignoring the expression on her mom's face that she couldn't quite read but made her heart hurt anyway. They'd never really made up after their big fight, instead following some sort of silent agreement to *not* talk about it, but Pluto knew her mom was still thinking about how Pluto said she wanted to live with her dad. Especially now while she was on the phone with him.

"Hi," Pluto said into the cell.

"Pluto Jean! How you doing, kid?" her dad's voice was crisp and clear and upbeat.

"Good," she said. "You? Is Sarah there?"

Another flash of *something* came up on her mom's face,

and Pluto got up to head to her bedroom. She sat on the floor at the foot of her bed. Even though her mom could still hear the whole conversation, Pluto didn't have to watch her reactions.

"Ah, no, she's, well, she's not here just now," her dad said. "But I'm doing good! Miss you, though! I keep forgetting to put the air mattress away, so it's just been deflated on the floor of my office, all sad and pathetic like."

"Oh" was all Pluto could think to say.

"An actual bed might be better, though," he said. "I heard you went back to your therapist, and that's great. I've done some research around here and think I've got a really great one for you to see, instead, if you want. Your mom said maybe you did. And I think that's great, Pluto Jean, I really do. I think you just need some space from your mom, and you'll see. I can keep teaching you D&D."

Pluto didn't know what to say. "Fallon wants to be GM next time."

"How about *you*, Pluto Jean? There's so much for you to explore here, still. It's time we had our own adventure."

Pluto glanced through her doorway to where her mom was standing in the living room, looking small and young and frail.

Her dad kept talking, but Pluto wasn't really listening anymore.

Pluto met Fallon on the boardwalk at the bench that sat between their families' shops. They hadn't really talked all that much since Pluto had snapped at her and said all sorts of things she didn't mean, but Fallon had texted her earlier, asking if they could meet up. Pluto responded almost immediately. She had missed so many opportunities to fix things with Meredith—she couldn't let that happen with Fallon.

Fallon had the Star Trek book she'd borrowed from Pluto sitting on her lap, but Pluto didn't mention it. Neither one said much of anything at first. Fallon was tracing the edge of the book with her fingers, and Pluto had all of her words trapped in her throat as she tried to figure out a way to apologize, to explain. Just like Mrs. McAuliffe told her to do.

Thinking about Mrs. McAuliffe made Pluto wonder if she and Sunny ever fought.

"I'm sorry." The words finally loosened themselves from Pluto's chest.

Fallon shrugged, still playing with the edges of the book in her lap. "I know."

"Mrs. McAuliffe, my tutor, she said we could read that book you lent me for my reading assignment," Pluto continued, hoping this connection would help ease them back together. "We just started it."

A flock of seagulls flew over their heads, and Pluto and Fallon ducked and covered themselves with their arms until the birds flew away.

Pluto sighed. "I didn't mean what I said. I was really mad at my mom, and at everything, and . . . I don't know. I like your haircut, and I know it was important to you."

"You said I wouldn't understand, but I do," Fallon said. "I get angry a lot, too, and sometimes I get so sad, because I don't . . . My mom doesn't get it, but sometimes I look in the mirror and I feel all wrong. The haircut made things a little better. I'm *still trying* to make it feel better when I look in the mirror."

Pluto put her hand over Fallon's, stopping her fingers from brushing against the pages of the book. "I really am sorry."

"Thanks." Fallon smiled, but it slowly faded as she quietly added, "Hey, Pluto?"

"Yeah?"

"You think I could talk to your mom? I had some questions"—Fallon paused, frustration all over her face, then took a deep breath—"about this book. I wanted to ask your mom questions about the physics and stuff."

"You can ask me," Pluto said. "I'll probably know the answer. Or we can call the planetarium hotline. They usually know the Star Trek stuff, too, and—"

"Actually, I lied. I'm sorry. I—That's not what I need to ask her about." Fallon exhaled slowly. "I really want to talk to my mom about the dress. You know, the one on my list? For Grant's wedding? I hate it." She paused. "Well, no, I like the dress, it's actually really pretty. But I don't want to wear it. I don't feel right wearing it."

"I can come with you if you want. When you ask her?"

"Actually," Fallon said, "I kind of wanted to practice first."

"On me?" Pluto asked.

"No." Fallon laughed, blushing. "On your mom."

"I don't want to wear a dress to Grant's wedding."

"Why not?" Pluto's mom sat across from Pluto and Fallon in the back of the pizzeria.

Fallon shifted in her seat. Pluto squeezed her hand and held it as Fallon continued. "I don't like wearing dresses."

"Well, why not?" Pluto's mom asked. They'd told her Fallon wanted to practice on her, and her mom said she would play devil's advocate. Pluto didn't know what that meant, but as her mom stared down Fallon with an intense, unwavering gaze, she was starting to guess that it meant she would be kind of annoying.

"I can't explain," Fallon said, her voice cracking.

Which also made her mom crack. Clearly, she was no good at this devil's advocate thing. "Okay, sweetheart, your mom is just going to want to understand. She loves you, right? If this is important to you, if this hurts you, she'll want to know that. Hopefully she'll want to listen. But if you really want to do this, you're going to have to try to explain. Otherwise . . . Well, she just won't understand because she couldn't possibly know where to start. So you're going to have to try, okay? For her, and for you."

"Okay," Fallon said.

Okay, Pluto thought.

Fallon took a deep breath. "Wearing a dress makes me feel not like me. Like nothing looks right. I feel . . ."

"Uncomfortable?" Pluto's mom asked.

Fallon had tears in her eyes. *"Wrong."*

Pluto's mom reached forward to cup Fallon's cheek, wiping her thumb at the tears. "Tell her that, Fallon," she said. "You tell her that, and you make her hear you."

Later that evening, Pluto's mom was making grilled cheese sandwiches. She hadn't defrosted anything for dinner and was exhausted from a busy workday. Pluto didn't mind. She liked grilled cheese.

She sat at their small kitchen table watching her mom grill the sandwiches on the stovetop, her hair pulled up in a crazy-looking bun, her pajama shorts and glasses on, as if she'd come home for the night and declared the day officially over. She looked young and carefree as she flipped the sandwiches, humming a song that quickly got stuck in Pluto's head, too.

Make her hear you. That was the advice Pluto's mom had given to Fallon, and Fallon was at home right now possibly taking the leap and telling her mom she did not want to wear that dress, no matter how pretty it was, no matter how much her mom wanted her to.

Pluto checked her phone to see if she had any texts from Fallon, but she had none. She hoped Fallon's mom was listening to her.

Pluto's mom flung a sandwich onto a paper plate and held it out for Pluto to take. "Thanks," she said, as her mom plated the second sandwich and joined Pluto at the table.

When Pluto didn't pick it up, her mom asked with her mouth full, "What's wrong?"

"I need to ask you something."

Her mom put down her sandwich and wiped her mouth with a napkin. "What do you need to ask me?"

"I want to paint my bedroom walls," she said. "I don't want the spots from the stars there anymore. And I want a new comforter. I like the stars, I do, but I want to pick out something . . . new." *Something that doesn't remind me of months of sleeping and not leaving them.*

Her mom slowly nodded. "Okay. We can do that."

"And I want a bedroom door again."

Her mom's entire body went very, very still. She opened her mouth, closed it, breathed in through her nose and then opened it again, and said carefully, "I don't think that's a good idea just now."

Mercury, Venus, Earth, and Mars. Pluto scowled, anger bubbling up to join the tightness in her chest. "Why not?"

Her mom looked afraid. Which hurt, but mostly just made Pluto angrier. "Listen, Shooting Star, it's just . . . not a good time yet. When things settle down, I promise we'll get it fixed, but right now—"

"That's not fair!" Pluto yelled.

"Pluto, calm down."

"Mom, please. I just want a door. I just want things to go back to how they used to feel. Before the diagnosis. Before that night," Pluto said, trying not to cry. "Dr. Collins says I have to bridge the gap between before and after, but every time I look at where the door used to be I think about that night, and I don't want to anymore!"

"Neither do I!" her mom said, her face red. "I think about that night all the time, Pluto. *All the damn time.* And I just . . . The answer is no. I cannot put a door back right now. Not when you can lock me out. Not when you can just . . . shut me out and *terrify* me."

Her mom stood, taking her plate and her half-eaten sandwich and throwing it in the trash. She braced her hands on the counter, bowed her head, and closed her eyes.

"I don't mean to scare you," Pluto said quietly. It was the only thing she could think to say, and it was true.

"I know," her mom said. "I'm sorry, I just . . ."

"I don't need a door," Pluto said, which was a lie.

"I didn't know what I was going to find when I broke

down the door that night." Her mom turned, looking at her with tears in her eyes. "I need time, Pluto. Give your medication time. Give . . . therapy time, and us time to just . . . figure this out. *Please.*"

Pluto wanted to call the Hayden Planetarium Astronomy Question and Answer Hotline and ask how long it took the scientists to decide Pluto should not be a planet. She wanted to ask her mom how long she waited before she broke down the bedroom door.

"We'll paint the walls," her mom said. "And get you a new bedspread."

Pluto looked away, thinking about the paint chips on her bedroom wall. She wondered what her mom had done with all those glow-in-the-dark stars. Had she thrown them away? Or had she saved them in a box somewhere, waiting, hoping, that Pluto would ask to put them up again?

"Okay," Pluto said.

"I love you, Shooting Star," her mom said, and Pluto couldn't help wondering if she and her mom were too different now. Maybe they just couldn't—wouldn't—fit together like perfect puzzle pieces anymore.

She hoped Fallon's conversation was more successful.

Pluto sat in the back corner booth of the pizzeria, staring through the glass doors, looking for Fallon among the people walking by on the boardwalk. The last time she'd heard from Fallon was a text that said, *I talked to my mom. Will tell you about it later!*

When she finally saw someone she recognized through those windows, though, it wasn't Fallon. Pluto sighed. The bell jingled above the door as Harper entered, with Charlotte and Meredith following, skin sun-kissed and foreheads sweaty.

"Hey, Pluto! Can we have some water?" Harper asked.

Pluto fought the urge to hide in the back and managed to nod instead. She climbed out of her seat and headed to the counter to get them cups of ice water, even though her mom was standing right there and could have gotten them herself.

"Hey, girls," Donna chirped, as Pluto's mom asked, "Hot out there?"

"*So* hot, Ms. Timoney!" Harper answered, groaning. "I might faint."

"You won't faint," Charlotte said. "We were hoping to just get some water and then go get ice cream to totally cool off."

"Oh, ice cream sounds so good," Pluto's mom practically moaned.

Pluto pushed the three waters across the counter. Meredith hovered for a moment before taking hers. "Hey, Pluto?" she said. "Do you . . . want to maybe come get ice cream with us?"

Pluto felt everyone's eyes on her, waiting for the answer.

"Just the one by the fun house," Meredith said. "And then we can come right back, if you want."

No. She didn't want to do that.

But also . . . maybe she did?

Maybe she just wanted to prove she was capable of *something.*

So, to everyone's surprise, Pluto found herself saying, "Okay."

Pluto was unfocused and quiet as they walked down the boardwalk to the ice cream stand, which was okay, because Harper was chatty, and Charlotte was a good listener, and the girls had spent the summer getting used to one another as a trio already. Pluto fell behind them, let Harper and Charlotte take the lead. Meredith fell in step beside her.

As they made their way past the Zamprognas' funnel cake store, Fallon was out front, chasing the seagulls away from where someone had dropped their zeppoles. When she saw the girls, she stopped, and Pluto lifted her hand in a small wave.

"Hey!" Harper called. "We're getting ice cream. Do you want to come?"

And that's how Fallon ended up with Pluto and her friends, a weird mix of old and new, of *before* the diagnosis and *after*, that put Pluto on edge.

When space debris crashes into satellites, the resulting radiation can cause the hardware to fry. When a new friend crashes into old friends, that collision can cause Pluto Jean Timoney's hardware to fry, too.

Harper asked Fallon a million questions. "Where do you go to school?" and "What kind of ice cream are you gonna get?" and "Can I get free funnel cakes?"

"I like her short hair," Charlotte whispered, which made Pluto want to tell Charlotte that only *she* could like Fallon's hair, because she cut Fallon's hair, and Fallon was hers, not theirs. Only she didn't, because Fallon seemed to be enjoying herself as she answered Harper's questions, and she laughed at Harper's jokes. Maybe Fallon wanted more (new, better) friends.

Meredith was the only one who seemed to be as uncomfortable as Pluto. She was quieter than normal and forgot to order sprinkles on her ice cream cone. Meredith always got chocolate-and-vanilla twist soft serve with rainbow sprinkles.

Pluto ordered hers with sprinkles and offered to swap with Meredith. "I know you like them," she said.

"Thanks." Meredith smiled.

But then Fallon started frowning.

Pluto suddenly had a stomachache, and her ice cream started to drip down the cone and all down her hand. "I need a napkin," she said, walking over to the napkin dispenser by the wall.

"Everything okay?" Fallon asked. The other three

were right behind her, looking at Pluto, waiting for Pluto to answer, and why did everything have to be so hard? Why couldn't she just get ice cream with her friends like she used to?

"Sorry, I just . . ." Pluto shook her head. "Felt weird for a minute."

Harper groaned. "*Everything* makes you feel weird lately."

"Hey!" Meredith snapped. "Leave her alone."

Pluto blushed, and Harper mumbled a quick, "Sorry."

And then they all fell quiet, and not the nice kind of quiet, until Charlotte spoke up. "I should get back to my mom. She'll be waiting on me."

"Me, too," Harper said. "I can walk you back to your mom if you want, Mer."

Meredith nodded, and the three of them gathered their things and said their goodbyes. Pluto missed hanging with Meredith. Missed Harper and Charlotte. But she was able to breathe a lot easier once they were gone—even if she hadn't *really* wanted them to go.

And then it was just her and Fallon, which is how it had been for most of the summer. "Oh! You never answered my texts!" Pluto said. "What happened with your mom?"

Fallon's face lit up, eyes bright, smile wide, and Pluto loved it. She wished Fallon could keep that look on her face always. "I was waiting to tell you in person! Your mom was so right, Pluto. I was honest, and I told her how I felt, and I tried my best to tell her why."

"Did she understand?" Pluto asked.

"Not really? She wants . . . well, she wants me to see a therapist, but not because she thinks I'm wrong, just because she thinks it would be good to have someone to talk to," Fallon said. "Like you talk to your therapist."

"So, do you have to wear the dress?"

"No!" Fallon said, practically laughing with joy. "She's not thrilled about me wearing a suit like my brothers or anything, but she said we can talk about options. That we can go shopping and find something maybe we both like. It's working, Pluto! My list is *working*."

Pluto wanted to be so happy. She wanted to laugh and smile with Fallon. To be proud of her friend, to be proud that her idea of making lists was getting Fallon somewhere. She wanted to feel good about the fact that Fallon took a risk and poured her heart out to her mom, and her mom did not turn her down, did not shut her out, did not make Fallon feel like she was wrong for being and feeling what she was.

But all Pluto felt was jealousy. It wasn't fair that Fallon's list was working. Fallon had cut her hair and did not have to wear a dress. Fallon checked everything off her list, one by one, successfully.

Pluto had not successfully checked a single thing off hers.

23

"Pluto, come on. You need to do this. We're nearing the end here, and you need to complete this if you want to go to eighth grade."

Pluto was not listening to Mrs. McAuliffe. She didn't care anymore that she was *Mrs. McAuliffe.* She was Lucy McAuliffe, and it didn't matter how much pretending Pluto did. This Mrs. McAuliffe didn't care about the *Challenger,* and this Mrs. McAuliffe stood between Pluto and the eighth grade.

It didn't *matter* if it was a sign that she shared the same last name.

Pluto had never argued with a teacher. She hated

getting in trouble in class. Even when her grades started slipping and she did less and less and less, she never misbehaved. She wasn't the type of person who misbehaved.

"Pluto—"

But maybe it was just the *old* Pluto who wasn't the type of person who misbehaved, because she couldn't stop herself from saying, "No. I don't care. I'm not doing it."

"I know that—"

"You don't know anything!" Pluto said. "And you told my mom about what I asked you about Sunny! Will my therapist tell my mom everything I say, too? This is all dumb, and it's not going to change anything, and I don't want to do it anymore. I don't want to talk to you anymore." Pluto shoved the textbooks and they fell to the floor with a satisfying thud. She wished she had something else to throw, too.

Mrs. McAuliffe sighed and pinched the bridge of her nose. "I'm sorry. You're right. But I promise you, Pluto, your therapist is not going to break your confidence. Not unless she thinks you're in danger or will harm someone or yourself. Unless she has a reason to think you aren't safe."

"You think I'm not safe? Is that why you told my mom?"

"I think you and your mom need to start having more honest conversations."

"Then make her listen to me!"

Pluto was screaming. She knew she was screaming, and still, Mrs. McAuliffe didn't yell back. She looked at Pluto with a calm that made her mad, because she wasn't Christa McAuliffe, she wasn't some sort of sign. She was a fake, and Pluto didn't want to be there with her anymore. "I want to go home. Call my mom and tell her I want to go home!"

Pluto didn't move to get out of her mom's car once they got to the boardwalk. "Come on, Plu. Get a move on."

She wanted to go home. This wasn't home. "No."

"Pluto, I don't have time. I was in the middle of a million and one things when you called as is," her mom said. "So, come on. You don't want to be at tutoring, fine. We'll talk about that later. But you need to come with me, the restaurant needs us."

The pizzeria didn't really need Pluto. Pluto just needed supervision. So, fine. Whatever. She followed her mom onto the boardwalk and scowled even more when she saw Donna behind the counter. "Why do you need to be here if *she's* here?"

Her mom sighed, frustrated. "This is a business, Pluto. *Our* business. Our pizzas and our customers and our employees and our inventory and our stock and our finances and our bills and I don't know if you've noticed, but that means it's our responsibility."

Pluto shook her head, "If you hired Donna, then—"

"Damn it, Pluto, you're not listening! It's *my* name on the door, and I hired Donna to help me when I couldn't be here when you first got sick, but that doesn't mean I don't need to be here!"

"Anna, maybe let Pluto go sit for a bit." Donna motioned toward a back booth, and Pluto looked around the pizzeria. It wasn't packed, but there were still plenty of customers watching. Kiera was carrying a large pie to a table, looking down at her feet as if she was pretending she wasn't there, either.

Her mom took a deep breath, trying to control the volume of her voice. "We are so far under what we usually bring in for the summer. We are so far behind."

"We'll be fine, Anna," Donna said. "Come in the back with me for a bit."

Her mom looked like she was going to argue (which, Pluto would, too, because Donna was kind of talking to her like she was a kid), but the bell above the door suddenly jingled, and Harper, Charlotte, Meredith, *and* Fallon came in, bringing their energy and laughter with them. They had sunglasses on their heads and stacks of tickets in their hands. "Pluto! We're going down to the rides. You want to come?"

Pluto's eyes narrowed in on Fallon. They asked her first? She said yes without knowing if Pluto would go, too? "I can't. I'm busy."

But then her mom was practically pushing Pluto out the door.

"Hey!" Pluto said.

"Go," her mom demanded. "There's like a month left of summer, you haven't been out there once, and you said yourself you don't want to be here anyway. Get moving, go."

Pluto wanted to scream. She wanted her mom to be supportive like Fallon's mom. She wanted her list to have something crossed off like Fallon's list. Fallon had new hair, new friends. Pluto had unfinished promises and failed half starts. She had no bedroom door, and a mom who just kept pushing her to *get a move on*.

"Please, Pluto?" It was Meredith who said it, her voice quiet and gentle, and Pluto had to admit Meredith's friendship was important. Her birthday party at the end of the month was important. Maybe she *should* go and start getting used to being with Meredith and her friends, so that come her birthday, Pluto would have something else to cross off her list.

But also . . . no. But also . . . *yes.*

"Okay, fine. I'll come," Pluto said. She avoided looking at her mom, not wanting to see whatever expression she had on her face, whether it was pleased or eager or relieved or angry.

Her friends were smiling, but she couldn't bring herself to smile back.

On their way toward the amusement park side of the boardwalk, Charlotte tripped on a busted plank and scraped her knees. She didn't cry, but she came close to it.

"Are you okay?" Fallon was the first to ask.

Charlotte nodded, limping a bit from the sting. "Can we just go a little slower?"

"I can give you a piggyback if you want," Fallon said.

Pluto scowled. The others all started laughing.

"Yeah, okay," Charlotte said, and Fallon hoisted her up onto her back.

"Hold on tight," Fallon said.

Charlotte did. Pluto hated it. Everyone liked Charlotte. She was nice to everyone, always invited their entire class to her birthday parties, and brought in Valentine's cards for everyone, too. If someone was upset, Charlotte was the first person to ask if they were okay. In all the years that

Pluto had known her, she had never heard Charlotte get into a fight with anyone

Charlotte was easy. It didn't take as much work being her friend as it did with Pluto.

Harper led the way, as Harper always did, and Fallon put Charlotte down as they both fell in step right behind her. Pluto walked slowly, in the back, trying not to look at Charlotte's smile or the way Fallon had to keep jerking her head back to keep her bangs out of her face.

Meredith slowed her step, walking with her. "You okay?" Meredith whispered. "You seem . . ."

She didn't finish the sentence, and Pluto didn't answer her question.

Pluto Jean Timoney seems like she's struggling with depression. What else is new?

Meredith's and Harper's moms waved as the girls got close. They were with Harper's little sisters at one of the kiddie rides. "What should we do first?" Charlotte asked.

Fallon glanced at Pluto and smiled. Pluto didn't return it, and Fallon pinched her eyebrows together as if she was trying to figure out what was wrong.

Pluto felt wrong.

She felt wrong as the others all decided on the roller coaster. She felt wrong as Meredith shared her tickets with her so she could ride. She felt wrong as Harper and

Charlotte took the front row, and Meredith and Fallon sat on either side of her in the second. She felt wrong as the roller coaster started moving, clicking as it climbed up, up, up, toward the highest point on the boardwalk. It was a ride that Pluto loved, had gone on ever since the summer she turned eight and was tall enough. Meredith reached for her hand, and suddenly Fallon was also reaching for her hand, and Pluto felt dizzy.

She closed her eyes.

"We're almost at the top," Meredith said, pulling Pluto from her thoughts, knowing that Pluto always loved that view. She was never afraid of heights, because her mom taught her how to love the sky. "Open your eyes, Plu."

When they were younger, Meredith was afraid of heights. The first time they rode the roller coaster, Pluto practically had to beg her. Even so, Meredith kept her eyes closed, her head buried into Pluto's shoulder, and their hands gripped tightly together. "Open your eyes, Meredith, it's so cool up here!" Pluto had said.

And, because they were best friends and Meredith trusted her, she did.

Open your eyes, Plu.

Pluto did.

She squinted against the sun, and immediately spotted the moon—something she and her mom always looked for during the day. The moon was the closest thing to Earth in orbit, and her mom had explained how because of its cycle, it was sometimes even brighter during the day than at night. She thought about pointing out the moon to Meredith, to Fallon, but she didn't. She kept it for herself.

They were almost at the top, and Pluto looked out toward the beach, where some swimmers splashed in the water and sunbathers sweltered in the heat. Keansburg wasn't the nicest beach—you could sometimes hear some parent yelling, "Don't touch that!" at their child—but it was home. It was familiar. The sand wasn't always smooth, and the water was never clear, but it was still theirs, just like the boardwalk that surrounded it.

Pluto breathed in the familiar scents and familiar sights as they finally made it to the top.

"Hands up!" Harper yelled.

They all did, both of Pluto's hands still held by Meredith and Fallon.

And when she looked out, ready to fall, everything again felt . . . wrong. The flutter of the pulse in her neck felt wrong. The ringing in her ears felt wrong. The way she couldn't seem to take a breath felt wrong, and her head was pounding and her heart was pounding and she was sweating and were they falling yet? Were they going yet? Were they just suspended at the top, waiting for disaster like in those seconds before the *Challenger* fell, before it split and burned and ruined everything?

Pluto was absolutely positive that they were going to crash and burn and everything was wrong and she needed to get off, she wanted to get off, but they were at the top, and they were leaning forward, and they were suddenly going down, and fast, and she had no choice but to go with it. She pulled her hands away from Meredith and Fallon to hold the bar in front of her, to steady herself. Everyone was screaming as the wind whooshed in their faces and the coaster went faster and faster, and Fallon and Meredith were shouting and laughing and Pluto was sweating.

Black holes were created when a massive star collapsed in on itself, destroying and sucking in everything around it. Pluto felt like that star, like she was collapsing in on herself and she was going to take everything—everyone—down with her.

When the ride finally stopped, Pluto practically pushed Fallon out. "Whoa, hey, what're you doing?" Fallon asked.

"Pluto, what's wrong?" Meredith added.

Pluto shoved them both away. "Leave me alone. I just need to go home. I need to go."

"Wait, we'll take you."

"Just leave me alone!"

She ran. Ran away from the roller coaster and the rides

and her friends. She ran even though her breathing hurt already, burned even more as she pushed herself to run faster. Her arms and legs had pins and needles, and her head was pounding when she finally reached the pizzeria, finally pushed open those glass doors and heard the bell jingle.

"Pluto, what . . . ?" Her mom was at the register, and there was a restaurant full of people, and college-aged employees, and Pluto didn't want anyone to be there. She wanted to be alone. She wanted her mom to know that, to have brought her home in the first place, to *leave her alone.*

"Take me home."

"I gotta finish up here, Plu, go sit—"

"Take me home!"

She was screaming. And she was crying. She was crying so hard she could barely gasp for air, hiccupping a bit as she tried to ignore the fact that everyone must be looking at her. She wondered if they were looking at her with as much fear in their eyes as her mom was. "Pluto, you need to stop. Right now. I need—"

She needed to listen to Pluto! She needed to listen to Pluto and take her home and not tell her to get a move on, unless she was going to take her own advice and get a move on to take her home!

Pluto felt completely out of control. She couldn't control her tears or her anger. She couldn't control anything as she ran toward the register and hit it. And hit it again. And again. And it hurt, because it was so heavy and hard—but Pluto hit it again and again because her mom was not listening, and Pluto was mad, and Pluto's hands were hurting, her knuckles were bleeding, and her mom was wrapping tight around her, so tight, too tight, trying to pull her away.

Months before, when Pluto still had a bedroom door, she and her mom had gotten into a fight. Pluto's mom said Pluto had been cranky for weeks, and it was true. She had been cranky and had been unable to stop feeling that way. Her mom smirked and made a comment about Pluto getting her period, but Pluto *still* didn't have her period. That wasn't it.

The weight on her stomach hadn't been cramps; it was something else, something Pluto couldn't explain. It pulled at her like a black hole, and she kept thinking about black holes all through dinner that night. And something about that had felt good. It was the first good thought she'd had all that week, that thought of absolute nothingness.

She hadn't wanted to eat, and she threw her plate across the room and her mom yelled and Pluto yelled back, and she ran into her bedroom and slammed the door and locked it. She picked up her cell phone and called the Hayden Planetarium Astronomy Question and Answer Hotline, because she wanted to create a black hole. She wanted to get sucked into one.

She wanted to be *nothing*.

"Anna, should I call nine-one-one?"

"No, just . . . just hang on a minute!" her mom yelled back, and she pulled Pluto into the kitchen, where Pluto continued to fight against her arms.

"Let me go! I want to be nothing! I want to create a black hole and get sucked into it so I can stop, so everything can stop! Let me go! I've failed at everything, I can't do anything on my list! I can't! I can't!"

"Stop, Pluto. Stop!"

"I can't do anything!"

"Let me call someone. What's her doctor's name?" someone was saying. Pluto didn't know who. She didn't care who. "Anna, please."

"I've got her," her mom yelled back. "I've got you, Pluto, please. *Stop.*"

She couldn't stop. She couldn't.

"I don't want to try anymore. I don't want to be here anymore."

"Yes you do." Her mom was crying. *"Yes you do."*

Everything felt too heavy. Pluto's arms, her head, her

body—all too heavy. She gave in, and gave up, and sank into her mom's embrace as her mom sobbed into Pluto's hair.

Pluto stopped crying. She stopped fighting.

She finally just stopped.

24

Pluto woke disoriented. It was dark outside. Her bed was warm; her house was quiet. She realized she was still wearing her jean shorts and tank top. There was no note, no medication, no glass of water next to her bed.

Her chest was on fire, and her hands were sore. Her knuckles were flecked with dried blood, and they stung when she flexed her fingers, and suddenly she remembered.

Pluto climbed out of bed. Her legs felt like rubber as she walked toward her doorway, pausing to lean against the frame. Had she been sleeping long? Did she sleep through an entire day? She didn't know, and she hated that. She hated that she could lose time so easily.

The only light on was the one in the kitchen. Her mom was sitting at the table, papers spread over it, her head buried in her hands. Pluto stayed quiet by the door, watching the rise and fall of her mom's shoulders.

Her mom must have heard her anyway. She looked up, her eyes red, her cheeks puffy. She said nothing.

"What day is it?" Pluto asked, her throat scratchy.

Her mom swallowed roughly, closing her eyes. "You only slept for six hours."

"That's it?"

Her mom brought a hand to her mouth, holding back a sob, before pulling herself together. She nudged the chair across from her with her foot. "Sit down, Pluto."

She didn't leave any room for argument, and Pluto was too exhausted, anyway. She took a seat and waited.

It took her mom a long time to say anything. "We should clean up your hands. I couldn't . . . you wouldn't let me when we got home. I . . ."

Pluto covered her hands with her sleeves and kept them under the table where her mom couldn't see them.

Her mom released a long shaky breath, her fingers wrapping around the edges of the table and holding so tight her knuckles turned white. "Where's your list? Do you have it?" her mom asked.

Pluto frowned, confused, but reached into her back

pocket to produce the list. She handed it to her mom, who promptly ripped it clean down the center. *"Mom!"* Pluto shouted. She stood, and her mom's eyes immediately went to the bruises and cuts and dried blood on her knuckles.

"I should have never let you make this list," her mom said. "I should have—"

"But I have to do it!" Pluto said, reaching across the table for the ripped pieces. "I have to fix everything. I went to the therapist, and—and I'm almost done with tutoring, and . . . we can . . . I'm friends with Meredith again! I can go to her party. I need to do the list! I need to try, I need to. You need to let me do it!"

"You shouldn't have to! It's making you feel like crap, Plu!" her mom said, and then she rubbed her eyebrow. She took a deep breath. Pluto did the same. "We need to start over. I need us to start over."

"Start what over?"

"Do you even remember the things you were saying? Do you know what happens when you fall into a black hole, Pluto? I *know* you know what happens!" Her mom's voice cracked as she started to cry in earnest. "I'm doing everything wrong. It's like that night all over again. I just want you to be happy. I just want you to want to *live*."

Pluto did want to live.

Didn't she?

She wanted to stop; she knew that. She remembered that. But that didn't mean—

"Mom—"

"If living with your dad will keep you from . . . I . . ." Her mom couldn't seem to stop crying. "Just . . . just tell me, Plu. I know now I should never have let you make that list, and I should have . . . God, Plu, what should I have done?"

"Why did you rip my list?" Pluto asked. "You don't think I can do it?"

"You never should have thought you *had* to."

"But . . ." Pluto didn't understand. "Then how am I supposed to get better? Dr. Collins said that I had to learn how to understand the new me, but how do I do that? I don't know who I am anymore. I don't know what makes me Pluto anymore."

Her mom was out of her seat and crossing to Pluto, wrapping her arms around her and pulling her close, touching their foreheads together, as tears continued down her cheeks. "I love you. I love you always, more than the entire universe, more than anything in it. You are my everything. That's who you are, and so much more, and nothing can change that. *Nothing.*"

Pluto was crying now, too. "I don't want to have depression. I don't want to feel like this."

241

Her mom pulled her into her lap, and they were both sitting on the floor, a tangle of arms and legs and tears. "We need to start over," her mom said. "We need to start over and understand that no matter what, you are the very same Pluto. You are my Shooting Star."

"No, I'm not."

"*Yes, you are.*" Her mom took a shuddering breath. "And I promise you we'll figure out how to make this okay."

Having depression, feeling anxious and sad and angry because of it, is not something you need to be ashamed of, her therapist had said.

"Mom?" Pluto asked. "Was Grandma depressed, too?"

Her mom held her so close, Pluto could feel her tears. "Yeah," she breathed. "I didn't understand it then. Maybe I still don't understand it. I miss her so much, but maybe I should talk to you more about her. It just hurts to."

"I'm sorry," Pluto said.

"No. *No*, Plu. You have nothing to apologize for. You've done nothing wrong," her mom said. "You and I are going to start all over. We're going to figure this out."

Pluto's mom called her therapist, after she cleaned up the cuts on Pluto's hands. Her mom was on the phone for a long, long time, shut behind her bedroom door where Pluto could not hear her.

Pluto didn't think it was all that fair, and she hovered in her bedroom doorway, anxious for her mom to finally emerge.

When she did, she looked wrung out. Her gray eyes swam with clouds from the storm inside her. "You and I are going to go see your therapist together next week," she said.

"Okay."

"In the meantime," her mom said, "tomorrow might be a good day to pick out your new curtains and bedspread. And then we can paint your walls. Dr. Collins thinks it might help."

"Oh." Pluto wasn't expecting that. "Really?"

Her mom's smile was tense. "Really."

So, the following morning, Pluto and her mom made their way to a department store, walking side by side straight to the bedding aisle. Pluto's mom let her take the lead once they stood in front of all the bedspreads. "I don't know how to choose," Pluto admitted.

"Think about what you like," her mom responded.

"Will you help me?" she asked.

Her mom looked down, shook her head. "I think you need to do this alone."

There were so many—superheroes and Disney princesses and designs in every color. Animal prints, floral prints, and prints of stars and outer space. Too many options. Too many choices. What if Pluto picked the wrong one? What if it didn't feel right? What if her room always just made her think about that night and black holes and—

"It's just a comforter, Plu," her mom said, interrupting her thoughts. "Just . . . pick one you think is pretty. Or extra soft. Or catches your eye. And if you hate it in a few months, we can get another new one."

Pluto nodded and tried again. She brought her fingers up to touch the fabric. She walked down the aisle, trying to find one that caught her eye.

And then she found an ice-blue comforter that made her stop walking. When she reached out to touch it, it felt warm and soft and comfy.

"You like that one?" her mom asked. "I'll hand it to you, that color is great."

"I like this color, too," she said.

It reminded her of Fallon. It was almost the exact same color as her eyes.

"Well, what do you think?" her mom asked. "Is this the one?"

Pluto smiled. "Yeah. I think it is."

The blue bedspread and matching curtains were bright against the light gray walls of Pluto's bedroom. Her mom knocked on the doorframe, getting Pluto's attention, as she stood there with a can of paint. "I found this in the storage room," she said. "Same color work for you?"

Pluto nodded and then turned back to look at the walls. She counted the thirty-two paint chips one last time. "Did you keep them?" she asked.

"The stars?"

Pluto nodded.

Her mom hesitated before admitting, "Yes." Her cell phone started ringing, and she put the paint can down to pull it out of her pocket. "It's your dad," she said, looking at the caller ID. "Here, you talk to him."

She looked at the phone in her mom's hand. It was still ringing, and Pluto was thinking about what her dad would say if she answered it. If he would talk about his plans for her to come live in that busy city, with a new bed in his office, and the promise of takeout and jazz and D&D like last time. A weekend like last time when Sarah understood things that even Pluto's mom admitted she didn't, and her dad let her sleep, and nothing went wrong.

But Pluto didn't like the New York City pizza. She

only enjoyed playing D&D because it made her dad and Fallon happy. She didn't like that the city had no use for stars, with the skyscrapers reflecting the sun during the day and the lights shining bright all night.

"Dad worked. I don't think I told you that."

"What?" her mom asked, as her dad's call went to voicemail.

"He wasn't there. I mean, he was. For breakfast and dinner. But he worked." Pluto shook her head. "But you need to work so much, too. The pizzeria isn't doing good. You said so. That's why you hired Donna."

"I hired Donna so I could be there for you," Pluto's mom said. "And I trusted her to help me hold on to both of the things I love."

"I thought you only ran the pizzeria because you had to. I thought you wanted to work for NASA."

Pluto's mom shrugged. "Dreams change, Plu. I love that pizzeria. I love dancing around with the girls to old pop music. I love the locals who stop in just to say hi. I even love the summer tourists, with their thick Staten Island accents. I worry about it, that's true. I worry I'll let my dad down. Running a business is stressful, and I can teach you all about that someday, if you want." Her mom held out a paintbrush for Pluto to take. "But you're more important—than the pizzeria, than NASA, all of it. You know that, don't you?"

Pluto took the paintbrush as her mom grabbed the drop cloths to cover Pluto's furniture. She looked at her wall, at the paint chips they were going to paint over. "Why does Dad want me now? He used to be too busy. He had his own D&D friends on the weekends, but now he wants me to be his D&D friend."

Her mom tucked one of the cloths over the edge of Pluto's desk. "I don't know, but I do know he loves you. He really thinks it would be the best thing for you, to have that change of scenery. He's just trying to help, how he sees fit."

"Do you think he's right? How do you see fit?"

"I thought that I could . . ." Her voice broke off. "But maybe I can't. I have to be at the pizzeria all the time. He makes better money, and you could see a therapist regularly. He thinks he could give you what you need better than . . ." She drifted off in that way she did when she realized she was saying too much, when she realized she shouldn't be saying what she was about to. "Do you *want* to stay here?"

Pluto didn't know what she wanted.

She looked at her mom, really looked at her. Her hair

had dark roots the color of Pluto's that she was usually quick to cover up. She had bags under her eyes like she hadn't slept in forever. Pluto thought back to the day she caught her crying in bed, to the desperate, hopeful look always present in her eyes. She thought about how hard her mom tried, how much she loved sharing the stars with her.

She thought about how her mom wanted to start over, to try again.

Pluto realized she wanted that, too.

"Can we watch the Perseid meteor shower together next week?"

Her mom blinked. She was clearly not expecting that. "What?"

"Like we do every year."

Her mom looked as though she was fighting back a million different feelings. "You sure you want to? Only if you want to."

Pluto nodded. "I want to."

"Okay," her mom said, and then pulled the lid off the can of paint. "Then, okay."

25

"You've reached the Hayden Planetarium Astronomy Question and Answer Hotline."

Pluto needed answers that her therapist and Mrs. McAuliffe and her mom could not give her. For seventy years—for longer than Pluto's mom was alive, for longer than Poppy had been alive, too—Pluto had been a planet. And then one day, in 2006, it suddenly wasn't. "Hi, my name is Pluto Timoney, I'm thirteen years old, and I have a question."

"Pluto! What an awesome name. What's your question?"

Pluto took a deep breath. "How long did it take for

scientists to decide that Pluto wasn't a planet?" she said, and then added, "I know the qualifications for a planet. I know how they decide. And I know a committee of astronomers decided in 2006. What I need to know is how long they took to decide. Did they take a long time? Did they change everything too easily? And how did it make you feel? Did you start thinking about Pluto differently?"

There was silence on the other end.

"Please tell me the truth," Pluto said.

And the voice on the other end did. "It was a two-year effort by the IAU. Do you know what that is? It's the International Astronomical Union. They came up with a definition of what makes a planet. The biggest part of the debate was actually public perception. People loved Pluto as a planet. No one wanted to see it gone."

"But they voted no anyway," Pluto said.

"They did. But only four hundred and twenty-four astronomers were allowed to vote. Do you know how many professional astronomers there are around the world?"

"A lot?"

"More than a lot. Ten-thousand a lot."

"My mom wanted to be one of them, once," Pluto said. "She would have taken her vote very seriously. She would have thought on it a long time. Did they think on it a long time?"

"They took right up until the very last second of the deadline for the vote. So I'd like to think they did."

Pluto sighed. "But it changed everything."

"Maybe Pluto was given a different definition," the voice on the other end of the hotline said. "But at the end of the day, its properties are still the same."

Its properties were still the same.

"Thanks," Pluto said. "That's my only question. For now, anyway."

"You are very welcome, Pluto-the-Person."

After Pluto hung up the phone, the doorbell rang. She let her mom answer it instead of leaving the comfort of her room. She lay back on her bed, on top of her new ice-blue comforter, surrounding herself with its warmth, and gazed at her newly painted walls.

The chips in the paint were gone; the wall looked as if the glow-in-the-dark stars had never been there at all. Pluto didn't miss them . . . but also, she did. All thirty-two of them.

"Mercury, Venus, Earth, and Mars—"

"These are the planets near our star." Pluto sat up quickly at the sound of Mrs. McAuliffe's voice. "See? I do know a thing or two about astronomy."

It was weird to have Mrs. McAuliffe in her bedroom. Well, *this* Mrs. McAuliffe. Lucy McAuliffe. The other

Mrs. McAuliffe had been in the books in Pluto's room for forever. "What are you doing here?"

"I wanted to check in. I heard you had a few bad days, huh?"

"I'm feeling better now." Pluto paused to consider it. "I think so. For now, anyway."

"Good *and* bad days. It's a lot to get used to."

Pluto nodded. It was.

Mrs. McAuliffe motioned toward the edge of Pluto's bed, and Pluto nodded. She sat down and looked around Pluto's room, at the bookcase with all the space books. At the solar system mobile that sat on top. At the wall, newly painted, where she would no longer find any glow-in-the-dark stars. "Would you believe I didn't know anything about Christa McAuliffe until I was a teenager?" Mrs. McAuliffe said. "Well, no. That's a lie. I knew about the *Challenger*, just not the specifics."

"I didn't mean to shout that stuff at you," Pluto said, feeling her cheeks grow warm. "I was just . . ."

Mrs. McAuliffe waved her off. "I hope I wasn't a huge disappointment. Big shoes, you know. And I've got little feet. Not Sunny, though. She's got huge feet."

"You weren't," Pluto said. "A disappointment, I mean. And I like Sunny. If I don't get to go to eighth grade, can I stay in tutoring with you instead of going back to seventh? Please? I'll work harder, I promise."

"I'm afraid I can't do that."

Pluto's heart sank. "Oh."

Mrs. McAuliffe laughed, which Pluto thought was cruel until she added: "You worked hard this summer, Plu. Did you not even notice? You'll be in eighth grade come September, if you're ready. Which I hope you are. Which you should be, if you and your mom go to therapy, and work together, and you take your meds."

Pluto's jaw dropped. She could go to eighth grade? She could successfully check off something on her list?

Could she *really*, though? Would she be able to go back to school next month, when she couldn't go in the spring? What if she did all this work but still was too scared and sad and tired?

"You're fighting a bunch of emotions, I can tell," Mrs. McAuliffe said.

Pluto nodded.

"That's okay. You'll figure this out. It takes time, and it takes patience, and it takes work. All things that, well . . ."

"Suck?" Pluto said.

Mrs. McAuliffe laughed. She patted Pluto's leg as she stood. "Well, that's all I wanted to tell you. I gotta get going, Sunny'll be waiting at home. Which reminds me . . ."

She leaned close to Pluto, and Pluto looked into her eyes. They were brown, like Meredith's. Like Pluto the (not) planet. Pluto didn't think she'd ever noticed them before.

"I know you overheard what I was saying to your mom. And, well"—Mrs. McAuliffe reached to gently grasp Pluto's chin, to make sure she was listening—"if you ever need someone to talk to, about your friend Fallon, about your depression, about any of it, my door is open. I know you have a therapist, but it never hurts to have a big support system. And I promise this time it'll be between you and me, *unless* I think you're in trouble. Okay?"

Mrs. McAuliffe wasn't Christa McAuliffe. Her name was Lucy. She didn't know too much about astronomy. She didn't have a husband and two kids. But she had a Sunny, and she had big brown eyes, and she had a good sense of humor and was a great tutor and was a *perfect* Mrs. McAuliffe. She was Pluto's Mrs. McAuliffe.

Pluto nodded. "Okay."

26

Pluto's mom was meeting with the delivery guy, but Pluto didn't want to stick around to help with inventory. She needed to see Fallon. She had a lot to talk about with her.

"Just to the funnel cake stand and back," her mom said. "And you've got an hour."

The moment she walked up to the funnel cake counter, Fallon's mom came to throw her arms around her, which felt nice. Especially considering she pretty much helped maim Fallon's hair. "Is Fallon here?" Pluto asked her.

Tommy answered from his seat in the corner, most

likely in a time-out of some sort, based on the way he was facing the wall. "She gets to go play games, which isn't fair!"

"Tommy, shush," Fallon's mom said. "She left a little while ago with the other girls. They shouldn't be far. I'm sure you'll spot them."

The too-familiar tight feeling came to her chest, and Pluto forced herself to smile before excusing herself from Fallon's family.

Is this what depression was always going to be like? Is this the Pluto she and her mom were supposed to get used to? The one who couldn't always be friends with her friends, but they could all be friends with one another? Did Fallon realize she didn't need Pluto, not when Harper, and Charlotte, and Meredith were so much easier to hang around with?

She missed the days when she and Meredith were a pair. She missed sitting around during the last days of school planning their birthday parties. She missed Harper's big mouth getting them into trouble, and how Charlotte was always too kind to tell her to shut up. She missed Fallon's eyes and smile.

She missed her friends. But maybe they didn't really miss her.

At the very least, they no longer needed her.

At the very least, they were better off.

Pluto didn't go looking for them. Instead, she walked back toward the pizzeria. But when she got there she kept walking, away from the busy end of the boardwalk all the way to the quiet side, to the visitors booth.

She didn't know how long she stood there, watching the boardwalk, a place that felt like home. *Here, on the planet Earth, on the Jersey Shore, you can hear the sounds of the seagulls and the tourists and the arcade games and the roller coaster. You can smell suntan lotion mixing with hot fryers mixing with salted air. If you shield your eyes against the bright sun that reflects off the ocean, you can see the buildings of the city where Pluto Jean Timoney's dad lives.*

"Hey!" Fallon's voice startled Pluto. She hadn't heard anyone approach, too busy thinking about those skyscrapers and how she'd felt that weekend standing in the center of them. "My mom said you were looking for me, and *your* mom said you hadn't been back to the pizzeria yet. I think I freaked her out, but I told her I'd probably find you here, if you were waiting for me."

Pluto glanced around, looking for the others, but there was only Fallon. "What?"

"This is our spot."

Pluto frowned. It was. "I thought you were hanging with *my* friends."

257

"We just did the fun house. Charlotte got free tickets from her dad's manager," she said, and then added: "She had one for you, but we didn't think you'd be around."

"Well, I am," she said.

Fallon narrowed her eyes. "Are you mad at me?"

Pluto sighed. "No. I'm sorry. I'm just . . ."

"Yeah. I get it. I haven't been much help lately," Fallon said, looking dejected. Which made Pluto's stomach clench. "I'm sorry I couldn't help more with your list. I can try harder, though? I promise I can do better."

"I'm not doing the list anymore," Pluto said.

Fallon's face fell. "Oh."

"But it's not your fault," Pluto added quickly. "You were a big help—you were the *best* help. Yours was just working so well, and mine wasn't. And my mom doesn't think I should do it anymore, anyway. I don't know. Everything kept going right for you and wrong for me."

"We have different lists," Fallon said. "That's all."

Pluto shrugged. "I guess."

"I wouldn't have been able to do mine without you," Fallon said. "You made me feel brave this summer. You made me feel . . . well, for the first time ever, I feel like *me*."

Pluto didn't mean to let the tears fall down her face. She just couldn't help it. "I'm sorry. I'm happy for you, I really am, I swear. I just really wanted to feel like me, too. You would have liked the old me. The me before depression. You really would have."

Fallon wrapped her arms around Pluto and hugged her close. "I like you *now*, Pluto." She pulled back and seemed to make a decision. "I didn't do everything on my list."

"Did your mom change her mind about the dress or—"

"No, not that," Fallon said. "I actually crossed something out. Do you remember? When I first showed you my list?"

Pluto thought back and nodded.

"I crossed it out because I was embarrassed."

"But you don't need to be embarrassed with me," Pluto said.

Fallon laughed, a small little laugh. "Actually, you're the only person right now that would make it embarrassing."

Pluto didn't like that. "Oh."

Fallon shook her head. "No, it's not bad, it's just . . . The thing I crossed out? I wanted to do something by the end of the summer. I wanted . . . well, I wanted to have my first kiss."

Pluto's eyes went wide. "Oh," she said again. There were flutters in her stomach. The good kind, not the anxiety ones. The ones that she liked. The ones that chased the bad ones away. The ones she got every time she thought about Mrs. McAuliffe with Sunny. Every time, well, that she thought about Fallon.

"I like you now, Pluto," Fallon repeated.

"Oh." It was all Pluto seemed able to say.

"Can I . . ." Fallon swallowed. "Can I kiss you?"

There were a million things in Pluto's head, a million different things she was feeling. But, for once, it wasn't that her chest was tight or her head was pounding. It wasn't that she was sweaty and jittery because she was worried or scared.

She was excited. (And, okay, a little bit nervous, too.)

She nodded, and Fallon kissed her.

Would it be extra cheesy for her to think she saw stars?

After they parted ways, Pluto couldn't stop thinking about that kiss, and what it meant, and what she felt, and what that meant, too.

She paused when she reached the pizzeria, staring at the front door for a moment before reaching a shaking hand up to push it open. The jingle above the door sounded louder than usual.

"There you are," Donna said as she leaned against

the counter, her voice quiet, but unnaturally loud, too. Everything seemed amplified. "Your mom's in the back yelling at Martin for making the entire kitchen smell like cigar smoke. You know how she gets. Go back and see her, though. She was worried when that friend of yours came looking for you."

"Okay. Thanks," Pluto said, and made her way behind the counter and toward the swinging doors that led to the back rooms and kitchen. She paused, her palm against the door, before turning back to Donna. "Hey, Donna?"

"I'm mid-count here, Plu."

Pluto tried not to roll her eyes. "I just wanted to say thanks. For helping my mom this summer. I know she needed you." She stopped, considering her words. "*Needs* you, I guess."

Donna looked up from the receipts in her hands, smiling, even though Pluto knew she must have just lost count completely. "You're very welcome, Pluto."

Pluto pushed the doors open and found her mom in one of her usual bickering matches with Martin. He was laughing as he worked the pizza dough. "Look! Your kid is here!" he said, and then turned to Pluto. "Your mom's threatening to dump her perfume bottle on my head. I didn't even smoke today!"

"Liar," Pluto's mom said. "I'm going to booby-trap the back door if you even try smoking one of those things on your break!"

Martin just laughed, continuing his work.

Pluto's mom rolled her eyes and motioned for Pluto to follow her into one of the storage rooms. "I actually came back here to see how many paper products I need to order this week. Help me count. Fallon came by looking for you; she find you?"

Pluto felt her face flush and said nothing.

Her mom read her expression wrong. "Did something happen? Is something wrong?"

Something did happen, but for once, Pluto didn't think anything was wrong. Confusing maybe, but wasn't everything lately? She always felt like she was at the top of the roller coaster, waiting for it to drop. Could she take that plunge? Could she go to school in September, and be friends with Meredith again? Could they go to the arcade next summer and challenge each other at Skee-Ball? Would Pluto want to ride the roller coasters with her and Charlotte and Harper? Would Fallon want to come?

Would Fallon always like her? Even on her bad days? (Would she always have those bad days?)

Would Pluto's dad keep calling? Would Pluto's mom

262

keep pushing and begging for her to get a move on and try to do better and be better and be Pluto?

Would Pluto keep changing?

"Fallon kissed me," Pluto suddenly said.

Pluto felt her mom grow very still. "She . . . like on the mouth?"

Pluto thought that was a stupid question. "Yes. On the mouth. And I let her." Pluto paused. "She asked first."

"Oh," her mom said, and took a deep breath before repeating it. "Oh."

"Are you mad?"

Her mom bent down to be eye to eye with Pluto, reaching gently to grasp Pluto's chin in her hand. "You listen to me, Shooting Star. No matter what, no matter if I mess up, or say the wrong thing, or make you do something you don't want to, the only thing that matters to me is if you are happy. I just want you to be happy, and to do whatever you need to so we can get you there."

Pluto swallowed the sudden lump in her throat. She leaned into her mom's embrace.

"You know what? I can ask Chloe or Kiera to do the inventory," her mom said, laughing as she wiped a tear off her cheek. "How about we go get lunch somewhere that's not the restaurant, just the two of us, and you tell me all about that kiss."

"Are you sure?" Pluto asked, not wanting her mom to leave the pizzeria if it was going to stress her out or if she really needed to be there.

But her mom nodded firmly. "We've earned this lunch break."

27

The best time to view a meteor shower is when the sky is at its darkest. Pluto's mom taught her that. She taught her about the constellations and the solar system. She gave Pluto the universe.

She woke Pluto up in the middle of the night, and they put flip-flops on and kept their pajamas on. Her mom popped popcorn, wrapped up their biggest beach towel, and the two of them snuck out, over the boardwalk and onto the beach. They picked a spot right in the middle, where the streetlamps barely reached, and it was dark, and quiet, and when they lay down on the towel and looked up at the sky, it was covered with stars.

"Do you like space, Pluto?" Dr. Collins had asked.

Pluto *loved* this. Loved sharing it with her mom. She always had. Before the diagnosis. And now, here, after it.

"Mom?" she asked, picking the scabs on her knuckles as she tried to spot the shooting stars.

"Yeah?" she said, eyes glued to the sky.

"Can I have the glow-in-the-dark stars from my walls? You said you kept them . . ." Pluto said. "I don't want to stick them back up, but I just . . . don't want them thrown away."

Her mom's eyes left the stars and focused on Pluto. "Of course you can, Plu."

Pluto took a deep breath. "Mom? Why do you think my list didn't work but Fallon's did?"

"Hmm." Her mom considered. "I think maybe Fallon needed to change, for *her*. She needed to do the things on her list so that she could figure out the person she needs to be, deep down. You didn't need to change. You *don't* need to change. You just need to learn—and so do I—what it means to deal with depression. Your list wasn't about that, so it wasn't the right list."

Pluto thought about it. "What would be the right list, then?"

Her mom rolled to her side, touching her forehead to Pluto's. "Let's think . . . Take your medication. Visit your therapist. Keep talking to your dear old mom about how you're feeling. Be patient, be understanding. Trust yourself."

"That's it?" Pluto asked.

Her mom shrugged. "I think so. I mean, it's pretty clear I don't know all the answers. But I think so."

"Will you tell me more about Grandma?" Pluto asked. "Will you tell me about her good and bad days?"

Pluto's mom took a big, deep breath. "I'll try to tell you everything. But mostly I want to tell you about how much I loved her, and how much she meant to me."

"Did she like shooting stars?"

"She *loved* them."

Pluto was about to ask more, about what else her grandma loved, and about her depression, and her life, and her mom's life with her, but then she saw it out of the corner of her eye. And then there was another. "Mom, look! There! The meteors!"

Her mom looked up, wrapping her fingers around Pluto's as they lay side by side, watching the stars. "There!" Her mom pointed as a few more meteors flew across the sky. "Make a wish, Shooting Star."

Her mom kept watching the stars, and Pluto turned to watch her mom. She was watching the meteors with a childlike awe, eyes wide, smile bright, that made Pluto wonder what she was like when she was Pluto's age, discovering the universe for the first time and falling in love with it. She looked so young, even with the dark circles under her eyes, the worry wrinkles on her forehead.

She *was* young. It was easy for Pluto to forget that. She was young, and depression, Pluto's anxiety, was new to her, too. And she was doing her best, even if her best was sometimes wrong, even if her best sometimes hurt, sometimes made Pluto want to scream and cry and push her away. She kept trying. Maybe now, with them on the same page, with therapy appointments on the calendar, she would learn. They both would.

Pluto sat up to look across the bay at the New York City lights that glistened on the water.

"Mom?"

"Yeah, Plu?"

"I don't want to live with Dad. I think I'd like to maybe try to visit again. But I want to stay here, with you."

Her mom grew still, eyes on the dark sky as the waves of the ocean lapped at the beach and the summer breeze ruffled her hair. Her chest rose and fell with a deep breath. "Good," she whispered, biting back a smile. "Then I'll do everything I can to keep you here."

Pluto rested her head on her mom's shoulder.

Good.

Together, they watched the meteor shower. And, even though it was a success, even though she'd have been able to check it off as complete, Pluto did not once think about that list.

28

Pluto took her medication. She visited her therapist. She watched the meteor shower with her mom. She was allowed to go to the eighth grade in the fall.

And now, she was standing by the entrance of the Runaway Rapids water park that was located across the street from the Keansburg boardwalk, a wrapped present in her hand, wearing her purple cover-up over her bikini, the same cover-up Meredith had in blue. Her mom stood next to her, holding a birthday card.

The line to get in was long and loud. It was a gorgeous summer day, but one so hot that everyone was itching for the cool-down of the water park. Pluto recognized some of the kids in line from school. Harper and Charlotte were up at the front, but the rest of Pluto's class—most of whom she hadn't seen since spring—were scattered, carrying cards and presents in various colors and sizes, waiting to get in to Meredith's party.

Pluto froze, her heart drumming in her chest. She could hear the rushing water on the inside, the screams of children zipping down slides in their tubes, the sounds of people running around and cooling down and shouting and laughing. She could see, out of the corner of her eye, some of her classmates noticing her. Whispering to one another. She had stopped showing up to school, stopped coming around, and did they know why? Would they ask her? Would she have to explain it?

Would they be okay with it?

"Hey, look, there's Fallon," her mom said, and Pluto breathed a sigh of relief, because Fallon knew everything. Fallon still liked her. Fallon didn't need any explanation.

"Hey!" Fallon said, blushing as she ran over to them.

Pluto smiled. Fallon looked thrilled to be there. Her eyes were hard to look away from, sparkling and blue, like Neptune.

Pluto's mom bumped her shoulder gently. Not exactly all that subtly, either.

"Are you getting in line to go in?" Fallon asked.

Pluto's hands felt sweaty and she wondered if she was getting Meredith's present sweaty, too. She wanted to get in line, and go to the party, like she did every year to kick off the end of the summer with her friends and celebrate her best friend's birthday. She wanted to say hi to her classmates, to go on her favorite slides, to jump and splash in the sunshine. She wanted to do this. She had worked all summer to get here.

But she also wanted to go home. It was too much. It was loud, and there were so many familiar faces and so many possible questions. She had that familiar tight feeling in her chest, a ringing in her ears, and she tried to breathe deeply through her nose but was only a little successful.

"It's okay if you're not ready, Plu," her mom said.

"No it's not," Pluto said, fighting past the lump in her throat.

"Hey," her mom said, bending over to meet Pluto's eyes. "It is. Remember what Dr. Collins said? One day at a time. Some of those days will be easy ones. Some of them won't be. I'm here to navigate those with you, but you're the pilot here, Plu. You decide where your limit is. If being thrust into a birthday party with all the kids from school is a bit much right now, okay. We'll get you there eventually."

"What if we don't?" Pluto said. "What if Meredith gets mad at me?"

"She won't be mad," Fallon said.

"Yes she will!"

"Talk to her," Pluto's mom said. "Like you've been talking to me. She doesn't understand. And that's okay! We're still learning. Give her a chance to learn, too. Okay?"

Pluto wasn't sure. Still, she said, "Okay."

Pluto's mom texted Meredith's, and they waved goodbye to Fallon, leaving her in line as they walked around to the back of the water park, where the birthday party tables were set up and Meredith and her mom were waiting. "Hi, Pluto," Meredith said.

Pluto handed Meredith the present. She looked back at her mom, who nodded. "I can't stay," Pluto said.

Meredith's face fell. "Oh."

"I'm sorry. I have to go home. I have to . . ." She drifted off. There was a lot to explain, and she didn't know how to explain it to someone who didn't know how Pluto felt. Who didn't experience things like Pluto did. "Can we just hang out by ourselves this week? And I can . . . I can try to tell you why, then? I can tell you all about my diagnosis then."

Meredith bit the inside of her cheek. "Just you and me?" she asked.

"Yes," Pluto said. "Just us."

Meredith looked down at her feet. But then she slowly smiled. "I'd like that."

"Happy birthday, Meredith."

"Thanks, Pluto."

Pluto and her mom headed back up the boardwalk to their car in silence. Pluto was relieved that she wasn't staying at Meredith's party, but she was also feeling pretty low about it. She wanted to be successful, and even though her mom was keeping positive about it, Pluto still felt like a failure.

"Can we stop at the restaurant quick?" her mom said, interrupting her thoughts. "I wanna show you something."

"Okay."

At the end of the summer, the pizzeria always made Pluto a little sad. They stayed open all year, but fewer and fewer people came when the weather started to turn and when school started, and all the college kids who worked there left (Kiera had said goodbye yesterday), and people got too busy with their regular routines. When the summer ended, it still smelled like greasy pizza and her mom's Taylor Swift perfume, but it looked, well, lonely.

"You coming?" her mom asked.

Pluto sighed and opened the door under the faded

Timoney's Pizza sign, the jingling bell ringing out and echoing in the restaurant. She didn't know what her mom wanted her to see, since it all seemed pretty desolate, and she was even more confused when her mom started walking into the back, toward the kitchen.

"Get a move on, Shooting Star. I have something for you to see."

She followed her mom through the kitchen doors and froze.

Along the walls and the ceiling, and throughout the kitchen, hung Pluto's old glow-in-the-dark stars. The door closed behind her, and her mom turned off the lights.

They were bright. And familiar. And filled something up inside Pluto, like seeing a rainbow after a storm.

"I know you asked to have them back, but I thought maybe you'd like this," Pluto's mom said, coming up behind her to wrap her arms around Pluto's middle. "I know you might not actually ever want them hanging in your room again. You're getting older and, well, things change. We know that more than anyone, huh? But I just . . . couldn't leave them in a box. Not when I can so clearly picture hanging them up with you, seeing that happy look in your eyes that told me how much you loved them. And me. I mean, maybe it's stupid. I don't know. But I just couldn't let them gather dust. It felt so . . ."

"Wrong?" Pluto finished for her, and she felt her mom nod against her hair.

"Yeah," her mom said. "Is it okay?"

Pluto could try again to go to the planetarium when she turned fourteen. She could try to go to school in the fall. She could repair her friendship with Meredith, explore her friendship with Fallon. She could take her medication, and see her therapist, and have Mrs. McAuliffe in her corner.

She could have her mom, learning with her, supporting her.

After the *Challenger* crashed, the shuttle program was paused for thirty-two months. A special commission investigated. They picked apart all the reasons they had failed—so that they could learn from their mistakes, understand what went wrong, and try again.

Maybe sometimes Pluto would fail. Maybe sometimes her bad days would be too bad. Maybe she would always have to learn how to deal with depression.

And maybe that would be okay.

ACKNOWLEDGMENTS

This book was a hard one to write. For a while, I knew something was missing, and at one point went so far as to add literal fire to the plot to try to figure it out.

The fires didn't last very long (thank goodness, could you imagine?), but it wasn't until I was out for coffee with my friend and fellow author Josh Levy that I found the missing piece. Josh, wonderful sci-fi nerd that he is, told me all about the Hayden Planetarium Astronomy Question and Answer Hotline. Josh, this book wouldn't be what it is without your passion for accurate sci-fi representation.

I'd like to both thank and apologize to the Hayden Planetarium Astronomy Question and Answer Hotline for my numerous phone calls. I do, however, hope so many kids find your number from this book and reach out with all their astronomy-related questions. (And if that's you, if you have a need to discover the universe, if you have an important question about the stars, that number is 212-769-5901.)

To my agent, Jim McCarthy: Thank you for your patience with me and my ever-growing list of projects that I email you about constantly. Your time and effort and brilliance means the world (and stars and moon) to me.

To my editor, Krestyna Lypen: There are so few people in this world I would trust completely with my work, without hesitation. You're top of that list. Even if you always make me do more homework (this time astronomy instead of soap operas!) than I ever bothered with during actual school.

Everyone at Algonquin: Thank you for always making me feel safe with you all, as an author and human and little anxious toad.

Liz Welch, you are (thankfully) still my Theo and my wuffenloaf.

Mom and Dad, thank you for bragging about me. Have I nudged my way into being the favorite yet?

To every single middle schooler who has reached out to me to tell me your story, I hear and see you.

If you ever feel like Pluto does, you're not alone. Reach out to a trusted adult for help. Otherwise, here are a few more hotlines for you:

The National Hopeline Network has trained counselors available to support you 24/7 at 1-800-442-HOPE (4673).

If phone calls aren't for you, you can reach out to the Crisis Text Line by texting HOME to 741741.

And, finally, the Trevor Project is a national 24-hour, toll-free, confidential suicide hotline specifically for LGBTQ youth. If you are a young person in crisis, feeling suicidal, or in need of a safe and judgment-free place to talk, call the Trevor Lifeline now at 1-866-488-7386, or text START to 678678.